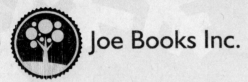

Joe Books Inc.

HarperCollins*PublishersLtd*

Published in the United States by Joe Books
Publisher: Adam Fortier
President: Jody Colero
CEO: Jay Firestone
567 Queen St W, Toronto, ON M5V 2B6
www.joebooks.com

HarperCollins Books may be purchased for educational, business, or sales promotional use through our Special
Markets Department.

HarperCollins Publishers Ltd
2 Bloor Street East, 20th Floor
Toronto, Ontario, Canada
M4W 1A8

www.harpercollins.ca

Library and Archives Canada Cataloguing in Publication information is available upon request.

ISBN 978-1-443442-83-1 (HarperCollins Publishers Ltd edition, Canada)
ISBN 978-1-926516-00-4 (Joe Books edition, US)
First Joe Books and HarperCollins Publishers Ltd Editions: November 2014
3 5 7 9 10 8 6 4 2

Printed in USA through Avenue4 Communications at Cenveo/Richmond, Virginia

For information regarding the CPSIA on this printed material, call: (203) 595-3636 and provide reference
#RICH - 592792.

DISNEY
FROZEN
THE CINESTORY

ADAPTED BY: ROBERT SIMPSON, ERIK BURNHAM AND JOSH ELDER
INTRODUCTION BY LEONARD MALTIN
COVER ART BY THE DISNEY STUDIOS
LETTERING AND LAYOUT:
SALVADOR NAVARRO, EDUARDO ALPUENTE, ALBERTO GARRIDO
DESIGNER: ERIKA TERRIQUEZ

SENIOR EDITOR: CAROLYNN PRIOR
EDITOR: ROBERT SIMPSON
PRODUCTION COORDINATOR: STEPHANIE ALOUCHE

SPECIAL THANKS TO:
STEVE OSGOODE, TONYA AGURTO, DANIEL SAEVA, CURT BAKER,
LEONARD MALTIN AND EDDY COLERO.

DISNEY
FROZEN
BEHIND THE SCENES

BY LEONARD MALTIN

Some movies are flops, others are hits, while a select few go well beyond box-office success and make a marked impact on our culture. Released toward the end of 2013, *Frozen* has had that effect on audiences of all ages and nationalities.

The film's success is exemplified by the enormous popularity of its signature anthem, "Let It Go," which propelled a Platinum-selling soundtrack, inspired countless performances on YouTube, and earned an Academy Award as Best Original Song. *Frozen* also made history by winning an Academy Award for Best Animated Feature, the first time a Walt Disney Animated Studio film has won in that category.

Whether you're a casual admirer or a devotee, I think you'll enjoy experiencing the movie in graphic novel style. It's an entirely new way of integrating the story, dialogue, and visuals from a movie into the realm of the comic book. It also derives inspiration from

BEHIND THE SCENES

Walt Disney's great legacy in the world of comics, which included adaptations of the studio's animated and live-action features in the 1950s and 60s.

Critics and pundits have tried to analyze why this film has resonated so strongly with moviegoers young and old, male and female. Is it that there are *two* princess heroines — or that so many people can relate to a troubled sibling relationship? Is it because the princesses are flawed? Is it the endearing comedic relief of Olaf the snowman and Sven the reindeer, or the contemporary quality of the songs?

"After having been around Disney for a long time, I wanted to do something different," says Chris Buck, co-director of *Frozen*. "Can true love be something other than the male lead's kiss? I was playing with the idea of true love versus romantic love."

Of course, that serious theme is woven into a colorful and dynamic fabric of music, humor, imagination, and often stunning imagery.

In truth, there is no way to quantify *Frozen*'s popularity. If there were a formula for creating megahit movies, everyone would follow it and there would be no failures. Something set this film apart, and that "something" is probably the sum of its many parts.

Yet just as *Snow White* was a film of its time, and *The Little Mermaid* reflected a later generation, *Frozen* is unquestionably a product of the

21st century…and the sensibilities of a female writer-director. There is no question that a modern woman like Jennifer Lee (who joined Disney in 2011, to work on the screenplay of *Wreck-It Ralph*) would have a different approach to both the male and female characters in a film of this kind. *Frozen* represents a healthy collaboration between Lee and her co-director, Disney veteran Chris Buck.

Gone is the practically perfect heroine, replaced by two sisters whose childhood friendship is ruptured by a cruel twist of fate. Elsa has magical powers that she can't control. Anna, shut out by her sibling and never knowing why, grows up to be a spunky, awkward but caring young woman with a true sense of wonder. With her spirited, optimistic, and fearless manner, she could never be mistaken for the simple, pure-hearted Snow White.

Lee says she wanted to create a heroine she could relate to. "I talk too fast, I'm messy, I'm sloppy, I'm goofy, I'm weird. We just felt like we could do that."

Asked if they were consciously trying to modernize the classical Disney fairy tale, Buck responds, "We are a product of our environment and our society, and that's what we put up on the screen."

Frozen also features not one but two heroes: one, a traditionally handsome prince named Hans who sweeps the naïve, unworldly Anna off her feet; and Kristoff, a mountain man who's so unaccustomed to dealing with people that he holds two-way conversations with his reindeer, providing Sven's dialogue as well as his own. (This subversion of the classical hero was first tried out in Disney's *Beauty and the Beast*, which sent a message to audiences, and its leading lady, that one shouldn't judge a book by its cover. Or to put it another way, a handsome hunk isn't always a hero.)

BEHIND THE SCENES

The foundation of any Disney animated feature is the story. Unlike a live-action screenplay, this is rarely the work of one writer but instead a team effort, wrestled to life through constant exploration and endless revisions. Experience is the best teacher in this process. Although Jennifer Lee is a relative newcomer to the studio, her work on *Wreck-It Ralph* was her baptism of fire. This is also the second Disney venture for composer-lyricists Kristin Anderson-Lopez and Robert Lopez, who contributed charming songs to the studio's 2011 feature *Winnie the Pooh*. Chris Buck has the longest Disney résumé, having started at the studio in 1978 and worked as an animator and character designer on a variety of projects before directing *Tarzan* (with Kevin Lima).

It surely didn't hurt to have the input of executive producer John Lasseter, the co-founder of Pixar, whose own studio emphasizes the importance of story construction just as Walt Disney did.

Although the movie takes its inspiration from Hans Christian Andersen's famous fairy tale, written in 1845, it bears scant resemblance to the original. *The Snow Queen* is the Danish writer's longest work, consisting of seven loosely connected vignettes. Each segment introduces new characters, settings, and motifs. (This hasn't stopped anyone from adapting it for stage, screen, and even ballet; there have been countless productions of *The Snow Queen* over the years, in many countries.) Boiled down to basics: Devoted young friends Kai and Gerda are separated when the evil Snow Queen abducts Kai, whose personality undergoes a dark transformation

because a piece of a troll mirror that only reflects negative qualities in people lodges in his eyes and his heart. Gerda sets out on an arduous journey to find her missing friend and tracks him to the Snow Queen's palace.

There are no royal sisters, no talking snowman or friendly reindeer. A kingdom isn't frozen and there aren't two men vying for a princess' favor. All of this was generated from scratch by the film's creative team, although Buck says, "We were inspired by that struggle and appreciated the overall message Andersen is sharing. We were also drawn to Gerda, the girl in the story who wants to save Kai. Her core characteristics— optimism, love, strength and determination—began to form what would become Anna."

Another component in the creation of three-dimensional characters is casting. The right actors bring a great deal to their vocal performances and inspire the animators and story team. Kristen Bell and Idina Menzel were ideal choices to portray the grown-up Anna and Elsa, because they are talented actresses as well as singers.

In the case of Olaf, the filmmakers were still grappling with how to portray the snowman when they met with Broadway performer Josh Gad, who won acclaim for his work in such hit musicals as *The 25th Annual Putnam County Spelling Bee* and *The Book of Mormon*.

Lee told me, "We were searching for the Olaf voice, and I couldn't write him. I knew he represented innocent love, but I couldn't feel how he would speak. Then Josh became available, and he came in one day. I brought in three pages; he did them, and then we played. We improv'ed and we talked and we explored. That session is the 'meet Olaf' scene, exactly; it was from that session. Then I knew him, and I could write him. It was so much fun and so easy." (Songwriter

BEHIND THE SCENES

Robert Lopez already knew Gad from having worked with him on *Mormon*.)

In some cases, songs helped express story points and character motivations better than dialogue could. The composers came up with the song "Let It Go" early on, to represent Elsa breaking free from years of repressed emotions. The filmmakers loved it, but it made them rethink scenes leading up to the moment.

"'Let It Go' was the first song that we all knew belonged in the film because it helped shape Elsa's character," says Lee. "It delivers such a poignant and powerful message about how she's feeling that we needed to back up and earn that song—to show how she finds herself in that place at that time."

The songwriting team of Anderson-Lopez and Lopez brought a modern-day mindset to this project that sets it apart from the songs of earlier Disney films. Their lyrics speak in the vernacular of today ("For the First Time in Forever") and the soundtrack's popularity is testament to their vitality.

With story and songs developing, the look of the film must be determined. Here again, many individuals are involved. Knowing that the make-believe kingdom of Arendelle is rooted in Hans Christian Andersen's Scandinavia, art director Mike Giaimo started doing visual research and found that he was drawn (no pun intended) to the look of Norway.

"We wanted to create an intimate world with an enchanting and dynamic setting that would be immediately identifiable for

generations to come," he says. "Norway offered a cultural backdrop we'd never explored before, and we thought, 'Wouldn't it be great to blend its dramatic natural environment, architecture and folk costume aesthetic?' It feels like a world from a classic Disney film, but it's completely new."

So it was that a group of Disney artists traveled to Norway to soak up atmosphere and fill their sketchpads. They visited villages and castles, fjords and glaciers. No detail was too small: they diligently researched hairstyles and costumes as well as settings. (They even brought back a CD of traditional Norwegian chanting—called "yoiking"—that became the compelling musical performance that opens the film and establishes the setting.)

But it would take more than artists' renderings to enable the movie's characters to interact with snow and ice in a completely credible fashion. The Disney staff did hands-on research to learn about footprints in deep and shallow snow, and how much of the fluffy white stuff would cling to a long skirt. To implement their findings in the production process, the studio's software engineers and visual effects supervisors fashioned brand-new, proprietary tools and technologies. An expert on snow from the California Institute of Technology was called in to advise filmmakers. That research helped the *Frozen* crew craft more than 2,000 individual snowflake designs.

Ice has its own unique visual qualities. It couldn't look like glass or plastic, and had to reflect light as ice actually does. The most difficult element in the film was the Ice Palace.

"For one single shot in which Elsa builds her palace, 50 people worked on the technology required to execute that shot," says Lee.

BEHIND THE SCENES

"And the shot is so complex that just one frame takes 30 hours to render."

It's a long way from the 1935 cartoon *On Ice*, in which Disney animators put Mickey and Minnie Mouse and their pals into a wintry setting: a much simpler task in those days before computer graphics and the audience's expectation of thoroughly realistic backdrops.

Perhaps the most impressive aspect of creating a film like *Frozen* is the way it combines so many ingredients: story and character development, dramatic staging, costume design, settings, visual effects, songs and background music, casting, editing, and more. When it works, it all blends into a seamless whole.

One reason it works so well is an update of Walt Disney's storytelling formula that came about at the time of *The Little Mermaid*. That's when a new team decided to approach each animated film as if it were a Broadway musical. Small wonder that producer Peter Del Vecho, songwriters Kristen Anderson-Lopez and Robert Lopez, and many of the principal voice actors have a solid background in musical theater.

Another reason is the continuity that exists at Disney. Director Chris Buck studied at California Institute of the Arts and, in his earliest days at the studio, learned lifelong lessons from one of Walt's fabled "nine old men," Eric Larson (as did John Lasseter).

There is even a link of continuity for the composer of *Frozen*'s dramatic score, the talented Christophe Beck. While attending the highly regarded film scoring program at USC in Los Angeles, Beck

got his first job on the recommendation of the head of the music department, Buddy Baker. Baker spent many years at the Disney studio as a staff composer and arranger, and provided the score for *The Fox and the Hound*—the first film Chris Buck worked on at Disney.

It may be intangible, but having such ties to Disney history can't be ignored or underestimated. Having people with this background working alongside fresh, new talent—unencumbered by tradition—breeds a healthy, creative atmosphere that offers audiences the best of both worlds.

Ultimately, that may be the real secret of *Frozen*'s success: presenting a classical fairy-tale story with a contemporary point of view.

Welcome to Arendelle

Anna

"I'll bring her back and I'll make this right"

Optimistic, loving and **adorable**, Anna finds
wonder and **loveliness** in everything.
She always sees the glass as half full.
She's a true **daydreamer** – and sometimes
she gets into **trouble** for that. When Anna
and her sister Elsa were kids, they used
to be very close: they played together
all the time, but one day Elsa locked her
out without any explanation – closing
the door of her room and of **her heart**.
From that moment on, Anna's desire is
to reconnect with her sister: she wants Elsa
to open the door to her, and wants to be
worthy of her sister's love.

Elsa

"I never knew what I was capable of"

Elsa is the heir to the throne of Arendelle. She's a **natural leader**, she's **controlled**, **regal** and **graceful**: everybody in the kingdom loves her. But she has a **dark secret**, a secret she hides even from her sister Anna. Elsa has the **power** to **create ice** and **snow** with her hands, but she's not able to control it at all times. She needs to wear **gloves** most of the time, otherwise she'd **freeze anything she touches**. That's why she shut Anna out – to protect Anna from her powers. She'll soon learn, though, how important it is to open your heart and let the ones that love you in.

Kristoff ❧

"Doesn't sound like true love."

Together with his reindeer – and **best friend** –
Sven, Kristoff gets blocks of ice from the
North Mountain and takes them to Arendelle
on his sledge to sell. He spends a lot of time
outside and he enjoys his work. Kristoff deeply
believes that sooner or later **people always
end up hurting you,** so he avoids getting
close to anyone – even to the love of his life.
Anna asks his help to meet up with her sister
Elsa. Two people in the whole kingdom
could not be more different...

Sven ❧

Sven and Kristoff have been **inseparable
life companions** since they were little.
This friendly reindeer is crazy for
carrots, and would do anything for his
human friend. Although he cannot
speak, Kristoff speaks for the two
of them, often putting words from his
own conscience into the animal's mouth.

Olaf

"Some people are worth melting for"

Olaf is the live version of the first snowman Elsa made when she was still a little girl. **Trusting, curious and always excited about the world,** Olaf has a **big heart** and is always ready to help others no matter what. Due to his **magical nature,** Olaf can divide his body into pieces – each of them moving independently – and easily put himself back together. **His greatest dream is to see summer:** he has no idea that heat could melt him!

Marshmallow

"Go away!"

Made by **Elsa** and prepared to **defend her ice castle**, Marshmallow is a **huge snowman** who is not very friendly towards unwanted visitors – his duty is to push away anyone who dares to get close to his creator. This is an easy task for him because of his **strength**, **agility** and his **terrible ice claws**.

Hans

"I would never shut you out"

Prince Hans of the Southern Isles is **fascinating**, **elegant** and **fun**. Last of thirteen brothers, he meets Anna on the day of Elsa's coronation. The young princess immediately falls for his smile and his **charming ways**: it is love at first sight!

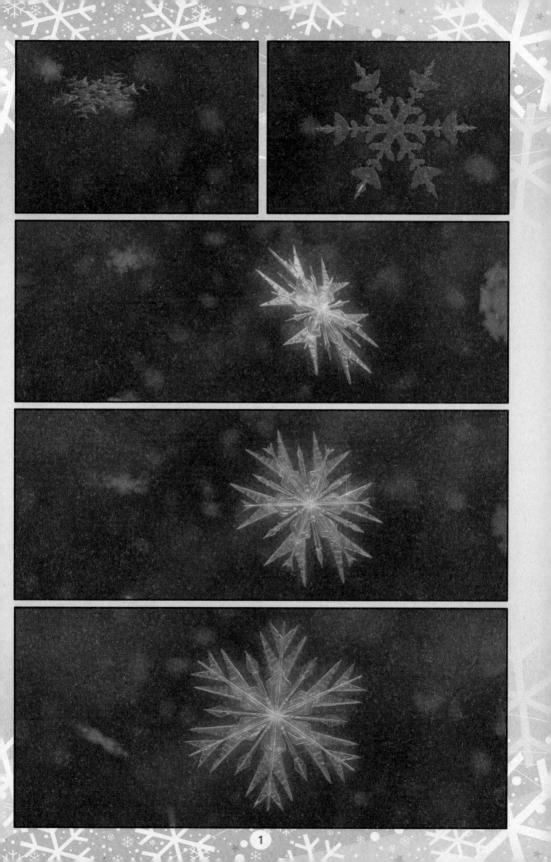

FROZEN

DIRECTED BY

CHRIS BUCK
JENNIFER LEE

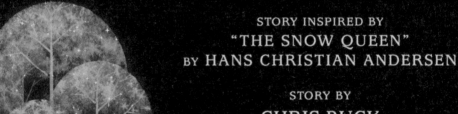

STORY INSPIRED BY
"THE SNOW QUEEN"
BY HANS CHRISTIAN ANDERSEN

STORY BY
CHRIS BUCK
JENNIFER LEE
SHANE MORRIS

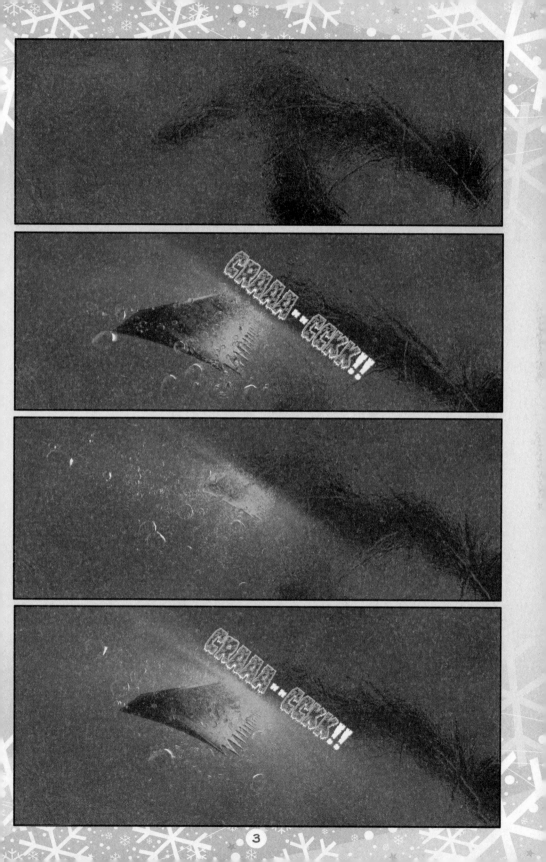

DIG DEEP, BOYS!

BENEATH THE FROZEN FJORDS IN THE MOUNTAINS OUTSIDE ARENDELLE.

HOW MANY YEARS HAVE YOU BEEN AN ICE HARVESTER?

TWELFTH YEAR ON THE ICE...

...AND I WOULDN'T HAVE ANY OTHER LIFE!

CUTTING THE ICE AND SENDING IT DOWNSTREAM -- THAT'S ONLY HALF THE JOB!

TO GET PAID WE HAVE TO GET THE ICE OUT OF THE WATER!

KRISTOFF! STILL TRYING TO GET YOUR FIRST ICE BLOCK?

HA HA HA!

COME ON, SVEN!

IT WILL BE GOOD TO GO HOME TO ARENDELLE. WE'VE BEEN AWAY TOO LONG.

FEELS LIKE FOREVER.

DO YOU HAVE THE SAW BLADES STRAPPED ON THOSE HORSES YET?

JUST GOT THE LAST ONE RIGGED -- THIS SHOULD SPEED UP THE CUTTING!

HI-YAHH!

WATCH WHERE YOU DRAG THOSE SAWS!

HI-YAHH!

READY, MEN? ON THREE! ONE, TWO --

-- THREE!

CRAA-CCK!

HAS THERE EVER BEEN A YEAR WITH NO ICE?

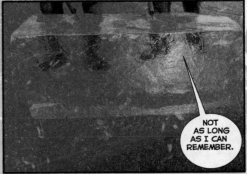

NOT AS LONG AS I CAN REMEMBER.

THAT WAGON IS ALMOST FULL -- BRING IN THE NEXT ONE!

FOREMAN! CAN YOU GIVE US A LITTLE LIGHT?

I CAN BARELY SEE THREE FEET IN FRONT OF ME.

HOLD ON -- I HAVE MATCHES HERE SOMEWHERE...

THE KINGDOM OF ARENDELLE...

NIGHT BRINGS SLEEP FOR EVERYONE WITHIN THE CASTLE WALLS...

...YOUNG AND OLD...

THE SKY'S AWAKE, SO I'M AWAKE.

SO WE HAVE TO PLAY!

GO PLAY BY YOURSELF.

OOF!

ANY OTHER LITTLE GIRL WOULD HAVE GIVEN UP AND LET HER SISTER SLEEP.

BUT ANNA WASN'T ANY OTHER LITTLE GIRL, AND SHE WANTED TO PLAY.

BUT WHAT COULD GET ELSA OUT OF HER NICE, COMFY BED?

GASP

THERE WAS ONLY ONE THING.

ELSA...

...DO YOU WANT TO BUILD A SNOWMAN?

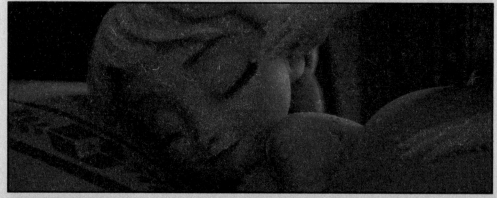

COME ON!
COME ON!
COME ON!

SHHH!

COME ON!

THE GIRLS RACE THROUGH THE CASTLE, GIGGLING AS QUIETLY AS THEY CAN...

...UNTIL THEY REACH THE GRAND BALLROOM, ONE OF THE BIGGEST ROOMS IN THE WHOLE CASTLE.

HEEHEE!

HAH!

AND THEY DID IT WITHOUT WAKING UP THEIR PARENTS!

DO THE MAGIC! DO THE MAGIC!

ELSA WAVES HER HANDS AND THINKS HARD...

...AND THE MAGIC COMES, GLITTERING IN THE DARK LIKE STARLIGHT.

OOH!

READY?

UH-HUH!

WHOOSH

ELSA'S MAGIC FLEW TO THE HIGHEST POINT IN THE GRAND HALL...

POP

...AND BECAME A GENTLE SNOWFALL.

THIS IS AMAZING!

THE MAGIC SNOW CONTINUED TO FALL...

OOF!

AND SOON THERE WAS ENOUGH FOR THE GIRLS TO FINISH THEIR SNOWMAN.

"HI, I'M OLAF!"

"AND I LIKE WARM HUGS!"

OH!

I LOVE YOU, OLAF!

26

THE WORLD OUTSIDE THE PALACE DIDN'T EXIST THAT NIGHT FOR ANNA AND ELSA.

THAT NIGHT IT WAS JUST THE TWO OF THEM.

AND OLAF.

FOR ONE NIGHT ANNA AND ELSA WEREN'T PRINCESSES. THEY WEREN'T ROYALTY.

READY? ONE, TWO, THREE -- GO!

HA-HA!

TICKLE BUMPS!

TONIGHT, THEY WERE JUST TWO SISTERS, HAVING THE TIME OF THEIR LIVES.

WHUMPF!

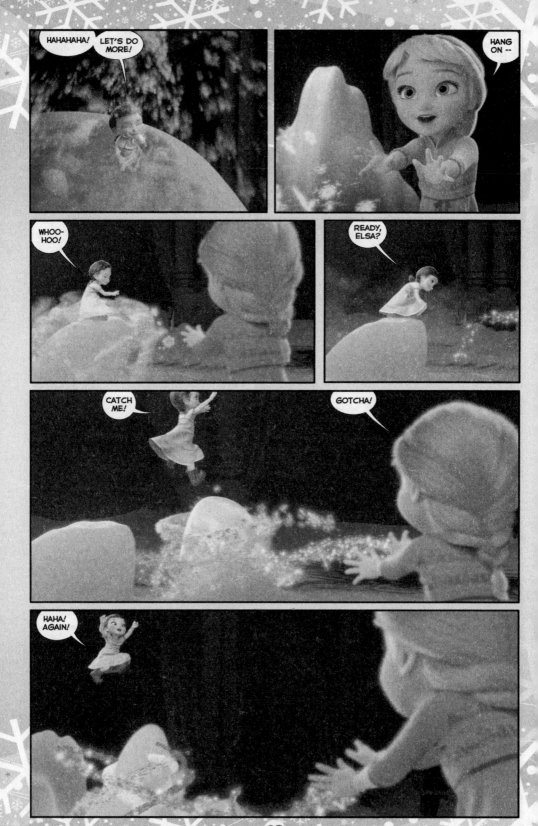

AGAIN! AGAIN!

OKAY, BUT...

JUST DON'T GO SO FAST!

WOO-HOO!

ANNA, SLOW DOWN!

WHOOPS --

WHOA!

STRUGGLING TO KEEP UP, ELSA SLIPS ...

...JUST AS ANNA JUMPED OFF THE HIGHEST SNOW PILE YET, STILL EXPECTING HER SISTER TO CATCH HER.

AFRAID HER SISTER WOULD FALL, ELSA REACHED OUT WITH HER MAGIC TOO QUICKLY, BEFORE SHE COULD FULLY REGAIN HER BALANCE...

ANNA!

FWASH

WHEE-HEE!

WHAM!

OWWW!

...WITH TRAGIC CONSEQUENCES.

UNNH...

Whump

GASP

ANNA?

ELSA WAS SCARED -- ANNA HAD BEEN HIT WITH THE FULL FORCE OF HER ICE BLAST.

ANNA'S SKIN WAS ICE COLD.

ELSA WONDERED... COULD THIS BE HER FAULT?

WHEN A STREAK OF WHITE APPEARED IN HER SISTER'S HAIR... SHE HAD HER ANSWER.

MAMA! PAPA!

NO, ANNA...

NO...

I DIDN'T MEAN IT. I DIDN'T MEAN IT.

PLEASE WAKE UP, ANNA. PLEASE

HER FOCUS BROKEN, ELSA'S CREATIONS FADE...

...LIKE MELTING FROST ON A WARM SUMMER'S MORNING.

... I KNOW WHERE WE HAVE TO GO

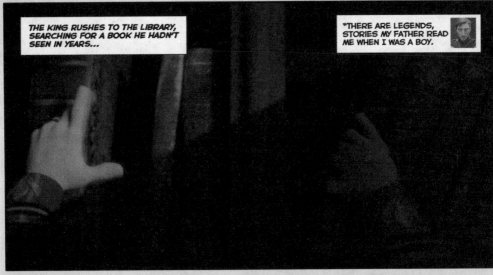

THE KING RUSHES TO THE LIBRARY, SEARCHING FOR A BOOK HE HADN'T SEEN IN YEARS...

*THERE ARE LEGENDS, STORIES MY FATHER READ ME WHEN I WAS A BOY.

I THOUGHT THEY WERE FAIRY TALES UNTIL HE TOOK ME DEEP INTO THE FOREST AND I SAW WITH MY OWN EYES...

SAW WHAT?

"THERE IS A PLACE IN THE MOUNTAINS, WHERE MAGICAL BEINGS DWELL...

"...HEALERS THAT HAVE SERVED OUR KINGDOM IN TIMES OF NEED.

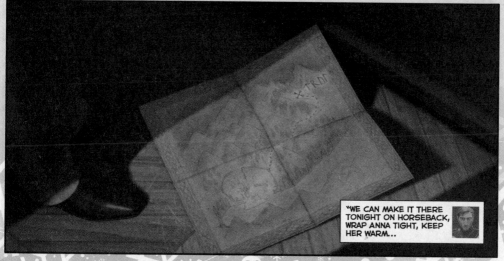

"WE CAN MAKE IT THERE TONIGHT ON HORSEBACK, WRAP ANNA TIGHT, KEEP HER WARM...

KRISTOFF AND SVEN FOLLOW THE
ROYAL FAMILY -- AND THE STRANGE
TRAIL OF ICE LEFT IN THEIR WAKE --
TO THE MOUNTAINS...

AND THEN... THE GROUND SHOOK, AS HUNDREDS OF STONES BEGAN TO MOVE.

RRRUMMBLE RRRUMMBBLE

RRRUMMBLE RRRUMMBBLE

RRRUMMBLE RRRUMMBBLE

RRRUMMBLE RRRUMMBBLE

WHOA.

THE BOULDERS SLOWED AS THEY NEARED THE ROYAL FAMILY.

AND THEN... THEY CAME TO LIFE.

IT'S THE KING.

KRISTOFF, SVEN, AND THE TROLL LOOK ON AS THE ROYAL FAMILY IS GREETED BY GRAND PABBIE.

YOUR MAJESTY.

BORN WITH THE POWERS, OR CURSED?

BORN. AND THEY'RE GETTING STRONGER.

HERE. HERE.

HMM.

YOU ARE LUCKY IT WASN'T HER HEART.

THE HEART IS NOT SO EASILY CHANGED.

BUT THE HEAD CAN BE PERSUADED.

DO WHAT YOU MUST.

SHE WILL BE OKAY.

BUT SHE WON'T REMEMBER I HAVE POWERS?

IT'S FOR THE BEST.

LISTEN TO ME CLOSELY, ELSA...

"THERE IS BEAUTY IN YOUR MAGIC..."

.43.

"-- BUT ALSO GREAT DANGER!

GASP!

"YOU MUST LEARN TO CONTROL IT."

"FEAR WILL BE YOUR ENEMY."

OH!

NO, WE'LL PROTECT HER.

SHE CAN LEARN TO CONTROL IT. I'M SURE.

AT THE NEXT SNOWFALL...

ELSA?

KNOCK KNOCK

ELSA -- PLEASE ANSWER ME.

WE COULD BUILD A SNOWMAN OUTSIDE.

YOU USED TO LOVE PLAYING IN THE SNOW.

IT WAS YOUR FAVORITE THING IN THE WHOLE WORLD.

NOW I NEVER SEE YOU.

PLEASE COME OUT.

49

C'MON OUT, ELSA. I CAN HEAR YOU BREATHING.

EVERYONE'S OUTSIDE IN THE GARDEN. WE COULD RIDE OUR BIKES DOWN THE HALL!

WHEE!

UH-OH! LOOK OUT BELOW!

MAYBE WE CAN GO ON SOME ADVENTURES TOGETHER!

HANG IN THERE, JOAN.

GREAT -- NOW I'M TALKING TO THE PAINTINGS!

ELSA'S BEEN IN THERE SO LONG...

I WONDER WHAT SHE DOES IN THERE?

50

52

ELSA?

"WE'LL ALWAYS HAVE EACH OTHER. I LOVE YOU."

I WISH I HAD MY SISTER BACK.

Three Years Later

SUMMER.

A TIME OF NEW BEGINNINGS AS THE KINGDOM PREPARES FOR A GRAND CELEBRATION...

WELCOME TO ARENDELLE!

WHY DO I HAVE TO WEAR THIS?

BECAUSE THE QUEEN HAS COME OF AGE.

-- IT'S CORONATION DAY!

...THAT'S NOT MY FAULT!

56

SHLURPP?

THAT'S BETTER.

I CAN'T BELIEVE THEY'RE FINALLY OPENING UP THE GATES, AGGIE!

AND FOR A WHOLE DAY, PERSI! HURRY, FASTER!

AH, ARENDELLE,

...OUR MOST MYSTERIOUS TRADE PARTNER!

OPEN THOSE GATES SO I MAY UNLOCK YOUR SECRETS AND EXPLOIT YOUR RICHES...

...DID I JUST SAY THAT OUT LOUD?

SNORR-RR-R

KNOCK KNOCK

SNORT HM? WHA? WHO IS IT?

IT'S STILL ME, MA'AM. TIME TO GET READY.

READY FOR WHAT?

YOUR SISTER'S CORONATION, MA'AM.

THE CEREMONY STARTS SHORTLY.

CORONATION! IT'S CORONATION DAY! HA HA!

CORONATION DAY AND I ALMOST OVERSLEPT!

EVERYONE WILL BE HERE SOON, THE ENTIRE VILLAGE!

DAYLIGHT! REAL DAYLIGHT IN THE HALLS!

I NEVER THOUGHT I'D SEE THE PALACE SO ALIVE.

IT'S JUST LIKE I REMEMBER FROM WHEN I WAS LITTLE.

IT'LL BE LIKE THE OLD DAYS -- ONLY BIGGER!

THERE'LL BE GAMES AND LAUGHTER --

-- AND SINGING AND DANCING!

ELSA AND I WILL HAVE TO GREET EVERYONE.

WHAT SHOULD I SAY?

PAPA ALWAYS SAID SMILE AND SHAKE HANDS FIRMLY!

BETTER PRACTICE!

MAYBE A LITTLE LESS FIRM...!

IT'LL BE WONDERFUL TO HAVE SO MANY PEOPLE IN THE PALACE.

BUT I'LL BE READY!

I'VE DREAMT OF THIS FOR YEARS. THE MUSIC, THE BRIGHT LIGHTS.

IT SEEMS LIKE I'VE BEEN ASLEEP MY WHOLE LIFE ...

"... AND I'M FINALLY WAKING UP."

I CAN'T TELL IF I'M NERVOUS OR IT'S SOMETHING I ATE...

...BUT SOMETHING'S FLUTTERING IN MY STOMACH.

I GUESS I'VE JUST BEEN ALONE SO LONG...

I CAN'T WAIT TO MEET EVERYONE!

WHAT IF I MEET THE ONE?

THEN SOME HANDSOME STRANGER WILL ASK "WOULD I CARE TO DANCE?" OF COURSE!

WE'D DANCE AND EAT. OH, THE DESSERTS! SUCH RICH CHOCOLATES!

THE DASHING YOUNG PRINCE AND I WILL TALK THE NIGHT AWAY.

HE'LL LAUGH AT ALL MY JOKES.

I KNOW IT'S CRAZY TO DREAM OF ROMANCE, BUT ANYTHING COULD HAPPEN. ANYTHING!

ANYTHING COULD HAPPEN. ANYTHING.

ONE SLIP, ONE WRONG MOVE, AND I COULD HURT ALL THOSE PEOPLE.

I WANT TO BE THE DAUGHTER -- THE QUEEN -- YOU ALWAYS WANTED ME TO BE, PAPA.

I'M JUST SO WORRIED...

IF I LOSE CONTROL FOR EVEN A SECOND...

EVERYONE WILL SEE.

IT'S JUST ONE DAY.

TODAY'S THE DAY!

WHAT COULD GO WRONG?

DEEP BREATHS, ELSA. JUST FOR TODAY.

GUARDS! OPEN THE GATE!

YOU CAN DO THIS.

I CAN'T BELIEVE THIS IS REALLY HAPPENING!

JUST KEEP YOUR GLOVES ON AND REMEMBER WHAT PAPA SAID:

CONCEAL IT. DON'T FEEL IT.

DON'T LET IT SHOW.

THE GATES MAY CLOSE AGAIN TOMORROW.

SO I HAVE TO MAKE THE MOST OF TODAY.

SO MUCH TO SEE! SO MUCH TO DO!

I WANT TO SEE EVERYTHING!

AND NOTHING'S GOING TO STOP ME!

OOF!

WHOA-A-A--!

MMMPH!

STOMP

I SHOULD --

I'M SO SORRY. ARE YOU HURT?

HEY. I-YA, NO. NO. I'M OKAY.

ARE YOU SURE?

YEAH, I JUST WASN'T LOOKING WHERE I WAS GOING. BUT I'M OKAY.

I'M GREAT, ACTUALLY.

OH, THANK GOODNESS.

OH! UH...

I'M PRINCE HANS, OF THE SOUTHERN ISLES.

PRINCESS ANNA OF ARENDELLE.

PRINCESS...? MY LADY!

SNRRT?

YOUR HORSE HAS MANNERS AS WELL!

WHAT?

WHOA, WHOA, WHOA, WHOA, WHOA!

OH!

I'M NOT THAT PRINCESS.

I MEAN, IF YOU'D HIT MY SISTER ELSA, THAT WOULD BE --

YEESH, Y'KNOW?

HELLO.

BUT, LUCKY YOU, IT'S-IT'S JUST ME.

JUST YOU?

HA.

BONG BONG BONG

...THE BELLS. THE CORONATION.

I-I-I BETTER GO. I HAVE TO... I BETTER GO.

BYE!

71

THE LAST TIME VOICES WERE RAISED IN SONG IN ARENDELLE'S GRAND CATHEDRAL IT WAS A TIME OF SORROW...

...TO MOURN THE PASSING OF THE KING AND QUEEN.

BUT TODAY THE CHURCH WALLS ECHO WITH SOUNDS OF JOY.

TODAY THE PEOPLE OF ARENDELLE AND VISITORS FROM ACROSS THE SEA GATHER IN CELEBRATION...

...AS A NEW QUEEN IS CROWNED.

A MONARCH TAKING THE THRONE IS A RARE EVENT.

SO ALL EYES ARE FOCUSED ON THE CEREMONY...

...ALMOST ALL.

IN SILENCE, THE CROWN IS PLACED ON ELSA'S HEAD.

NEXT, SHE'LL BE PRESENTED WITH THE ORB AND SCEPTER... AND THE CEREMONY WILL BE COMPLETE. SHE WILL BE QUEEN...

...AND EVERYTHING WILL GO BACK TO NORMAL.

AHEM...

YOUR MAJESTY... THE GLOVES...

ELSA HESITATED...

...BUT ONLY FOR A MOMENT.

SEM HON HELDR

INUM HELGUM EIGNUM

OK KRÝND Í ÞESSUM HELGA STAÐ EK TÉ FRAM FYRIR YÐR.

"AS SHE HOLDS THE TRADITIONAL RELICS AND IS CROWNED IN THIS PLACE, ALL RISE..."

ELSA COULD FEEL HER POWER COMING TO LIFE... THE SCEPTER AND ORB CHILLED IN HER HANDS. ICE CRYSTALS HAD ALREADY FORMED ON THE METAL.

GASP!

...BUT THANKFULLY, ELSA SEEMED TO BE THE ONLY ONE WHO NOTICED.

THE NEW QUEEN RETURNED THE SYMBOLS OF HER REIGN TO THE BISHOP, AND PUT HER GLOVES BACK ON...

...BEFORE ANYONE WAS THE WISER.

QUEEN ELSA OF ARENDELLE!

...I PRESENT QUEEN ELSA OF ARENDELLE!

QUEEN ELSA OF ARENDELLE!

IT'S A JOY TO SEE THE PALACE ALIVE AGAIN.

YES -- THE GATES WERE CLOSED FAR TOO LONG.

HAS ANYONE SEEN THE QUEEN?

PRINCESS ANNA LOOKED SO LOVELY!

THE QUEEN LOOKS SO MUCH LIKE HER MOTHER!

I WONDER IF THE QUEEN WILL SPEAK TONIGHT?

I HOPE SO. WHAT A STORY TO TELL BACK HOME.

QUEEN ELSA OF ARENDELLE.

PRINCESS ANNA OF ARENDELLE.

OH!

AHEM.

HERE? ARE YOU SURE?

BECAUSE I DON'T THINK I'M SUPPOSED TO --

·77·

SO, THIS IS WHAT A PARTY LOOKS LIKE.

IT'S WARMER THAN I THOUGHT.

AND WHAT IS THAT AMAZING SMELL?

SNIFFFFFFFF

...CHOCOLATE!

I--

YOUR MAJESTY.

THE DUKE OF WEASELTOWN!

WESEL**TON**. THE DUKE OF WESELTON!

YOUR MAJESTY.

AS YOUR CLOSEST PARTNER IN TRADE, IT SEEMS ONLY FITTING--

--THAT I OFFER YOU YOUR FIRST DANCE AS QUEEN.

SHRRRIPPP

SNRRRT!

SHH!

THANK YOU... ONLY I DON'T DANCE.

OH...?

BUT MY SISTER DOES.

WHAT?

LUCKY YOU...

OH, I DON'T THINK...

IF YOU SWOON, LET ME KNOW, I'LL CATCH YOU!

SORRY.

I'M LIKE AN AGILE PEACOCK!

ER --

GOBBLE GOBBLE!

THEY DON'T CALL ME THE LITTLE DIPPER FOR NOTHING!

SNORT GIGGLE

YOU DANCE DIVINELY, YOUR HIGHNESS!

GIGGLE

LIKE A CHICKEN... WITH THE FACE OF A MONKEY...

I FLY!

ANNA SMILES, HAPPY TO SEE THE PRINCE AGAIN, AND EVEN HAPPIER TO DANCE WITH SOMEONE THAT DOESN'T HAVE THE FACE OF A MONKEY.

THEY DANCE...

...AND THEN THEY TALK.

...I OFTEN HAD THE WHOLE PARLOR TO MYSELF TO SLIDE AS FAST AS I COULD -- WHOOSH --

-- WHOOSH -- OOPS!

SMACK

MMFPF

HAHAHAHA

...YOUR PHYSIQUE HELPS, I'M SURE.

WHAT'S THAT STREAK?

I WAS BORN WITH IT...

...ALTHOUGH I DREAMT I WAS KISSED BY A TROLL.

I LIKE IT.

YEAH, EAT THE WHOLE THING! YOU GOT IT.

MMMPH. THAT'S GOOD. REMINDS ME OF MY FAVORITE SANDWICH.

SO YOU HAVE HOW MANY BROTHERS?

TWELVE OLDER BROTHERS. THREE OF THEM PRETENDED I WAS INVISIBLE... LITERALLY... FOR TWO YEARS.

THAT'S HORRIBLE

IT'S WHAT BROTHERS DO.

...AND SISTERS.

ELSA AND I WERE REALLY CLOSE WHEN WE WERE LITTLE.

ONE DAY SHE JUST SHUT ME OUT, AND I NEVER KNEW WHY.

I WOULD NEVER SHUT YOU OUT.

OKAY, CAN I JUST SAY SOMETHING CRAZY?

I LOVE CRAZY.

PEOPLE HAVE BEEN SHUTTING DOORS IN MY FACE MY WHOLE LIFE.

YOU'VE OPENED A DOOR TO ME.

THAT'S AMAZING! I WAS JUST GOING TO SAY...

...THAT I FELT THAT WAY TOO.

I'VE NEVER QUITE BELONGED. NEVER QUITE FIT IN.

THIS MIGHT BE THE PARTY TALKING...

...OR MAYBE I OVERDID IT ON THE FONDUE...

BUT I FEEL I BELONG HERE. WITH YOU.

I LOOK INTO YOUR EYES...

AND I LOSE MYSELF.

IT'S HARD TO BELIEVE.

WHAT IS?

HOW WE ALWAYS SEEM TO KNOW --

--WHAT THE OTHER PERSON IS GOING TO SAY?

EXACTLY!

I'VE NEVER KNOWN ANYONE

WHO GETS ME THE WAY YOU DO.

JINX! DOUBLE JINX!

HOW DO YOU EXPLAIN THIS PERFECT HARMONY?

MY LIFE IS SO MUCH BETTER —

SINCE...

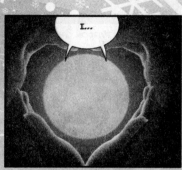

I...

MET YOU!

CAN I SAY SOMETHING CRAZY...?

WILL YOU MARRY ME?

CAN I JUST SAY SOMETHING EVEN CRAZIER?

YES.

"EXCUSE ME! PARDON ME! IN A HURRY!"

OOPS! PARDON. SORRY. CAN WE JUST GET AROUND YOU THERE?

THANK YOU. OH, THERE SHE IS. ELSA!

I MEAN... QUEEN... ME AGAIN.

UM. MAY I PRESENT PRINCE HANS OF THE SOUTHERN ISLES.

YOUR MAJESTY.

OF COURSE, WE'LL HAVE SOUP, ROAST, AND ICE CREAM AND THEN -- WAIT. WOULD WE LIVE HERE?

HERE?

ABSOLUTELY!

ANNA--

OH, WE CAN INVITE ALL TWELVE OF YOUR BROTHERS TO STAY WITH US --

WHAT? NO, NO, NO, NO, NO.

I DON'T KNOW. SOME OF THEM MUST --

WAIT. SLOW DOWN. NO ONE'S BROTHERS ARE STAYING HERE.

NO ONE IS GETTING MARRIED.

WAIT, WHAT?

MAY I TALK TO YOU, ANNA, PLEASE. ALONE.

NO. WHATEVER YOU HAVE TO SAY, YOU-YOU CAN SAY TO BOTH OF US.

FINE. YOU CAN'T MARRY A MAN YOU JUST MET.

YOU CAN IF IT'S TRUE LOVE.

ANNA, WHAT DO YOU KNOW ABOUT TRUE LOVE?

MORE THAN YOU.

YOU ASKED FOR MY BLESSING, BUT MY ANSWER IS NO.

THE PARTY IS OVER. CLOSE THE GATES.

WHAT?

ELSA, NO. WAIT!

LET GO OF MY GLOVE!

ELSA, PLEASE. PLEASE. I CAN'T LIVE LIKE THIS ANYMORE.

...THEN LEAVE.

...WHAT DID I EVER DO TO YOU?!

ENOUGH, ANNA

ELSA TURNED TO LEAVE, AFRAID HER POWERS MIGHT SUDDENLY RUN OUT OF CONTROL.

BUT ANNA WASN'T DONE WITH HER YET.

NO, WHY?

WHY DO YOU SHUT ME OUT?

WHY DO YOU SHUT THE WORLD OUT?

WHAT ARE YOU SO AFRAID OF?

CRACKLLLLLL

...SORCERY. I KNEW THERE WAS SOMETHING DUBIOUS GOING ON HERE.

ELSA...?

HER POWER WAS FINALLY REVEALED. IT WAS ELSA'S GREATEST FEAR COME TO LIFE.

SHE DIDN'T KNOW WHAT TO SAY OR DO...

...SO SHE RAN.

OH, ELSA.

YOUR MAJESTY? ARE YOU ALL RIGHT?

...NO...

ELSA BACKED AWAY FROM THE CONCERNED WOMAN. SHE STILL HOPED TO ESCAPE BEFORE ANYONE ELSE SAW HER POWER.

KRRRRIKK

BUT SHE BACKED INTO THE FOUNTAIN, WHERE HER BARE HAND TOUCHED THE WET STONE...

...AND FROZE THE FOUNTAIN'S SPOUT INTO SOLID ICE IN FRONT OF EVERYONE.

KRRAAKKAAKAKK

ELSA, WAIT!
PLEASE!

ELSA HEARD HER SISTER,
AND RAN EVEN FASTER. OUT
OF THE CASTLE, ELSA RAN...

...OUT OF ARENDELLE...

GASP

...STOPPING WHEN SHE
REACHED THE FJORD.

ELSA!

PLEASE, COME BACK!

THE WATER BLOCKED ELSA'S PATH -- BUT IT WAS ONLY WATER, SHE REALIZED.

AND WATER...

KRRAAAKKKK

...BECOMES ICE.

AS SHE HAD WITH THE FOUNTAIN, ELSA FROZE OVER THE FJORD WITH HER POWER AND KEPT ON, LEAVING ARENDELLE - AND ANNA - BEHIND.

ELSA, COME BACK!

ANNA!

NO.

ELSA! ELSA!!

ANNA... LOOK....

"... THE FJORD."

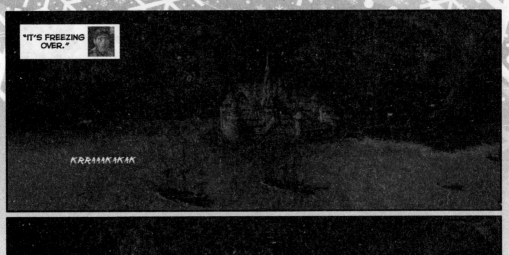

SHE NEARLY KILLED ME.

YOU SLIPPED ON ICE.

HER ICE!

IT WAS AN ACCIDENT. SHE WAS SCARED. SHE DIDN'T MEAN ANY OF THIS....

TONIGHT WAS MY FAULT. I PUSHED HER. SO I'M THE ONE THAT NEEDS TO GO AFTER HER.

YES. FINE. DO.

WHAT?

KAI, BRING ME MY HORSE, PLEASE.

ANNA, NO. IT'S TOO DANGEROUS.

ELSA'S NOT DANGEROUS. I'LL BRING HER BACK, AND I'LL MAKE THIS RIGHT.

THEY TOLD ME NOT TO LET THEM SEE.

THEY TOLD ME TO HIDE WHAT I WAS...

...WHAT I COULD DO.

BUT THERE'S NO MORE HIDING NOW.

I CAN FINALLY BE...

...FREE.

WHOOOSH!

NO MORE HOLDING BACK.

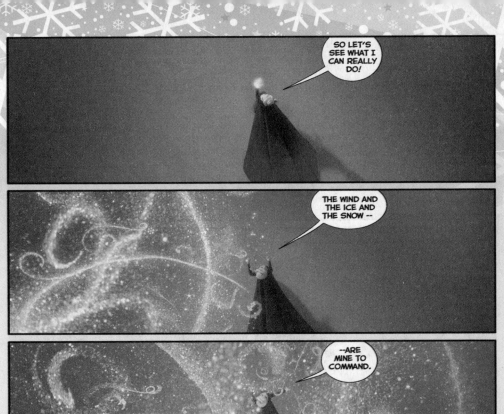

SO LET'S SEE WHAT I CAN REALLY DO!

THE WIND AND THE ICE AND THE SNOW --

--ARE MINE TO COMMAND.

FOR THE FIRST TIME IN MY LIFE...

...I'M FINALLY FREE!

WHOOSH

IT DOESN'T MATTER WHAT OTHER PEOPLE THINK

NOT ANYMORE.

SO LET THE WIND BLOW AND THE SNOW FALL!

BESIDES, I'VE ALWAYS LIKED THE COLD.

FROM WAY UP HERE...

...EVERYTHING LOOKS SO... DIFFERENT.

IT'S LIKE I'M SEEING CLEARLY FOR THE FIRST TIME.

A STAIRCASE OF PURE ICE BEGAN TO TAKE SHAPE.

ONE THAT WOULD TAKE HER EVER HIGHER INTO THE MOUNTAINS.

THIS IS INCREDIBLE!

WHY WAS I HOLDING BACK ALL THOSE YEARS?

NEVER, EVER

NEVER, EVER AGAIN!

ICE CRYSTALS SHIMMER AS THEY SWIRL AND DANCE IN THE MOONLIGHT.

ELSA'S POWER SENDS COLUMNS OF ICE SOARING UP FROM THE GROUND...

...UNTIL AROUND HER STANDS A GLORIOUS ICE PALACE.

THIS IS MY HOME NOW.

AND HERE...

...I CAN FINALLY BE MYSELF.

THE OLD ME...

...IS GONE.

NO MORE HIDING IN THE SHADOWS.

I'M GOING TO STAND IN THE LIGHT!

I TRIED TO BE WHAT THEY WANTED ME TO BE.

BUT NO MORE!

120

MEANWHILE, IN A VALLEY FAR FROM THE MOUNTAIN...

ELSA! ELSA! IT'S ME, ANNA... YOUR SISTER WHO DIDN'T MEAN TO MAKE YOU FREEZE THE SUMMER.

I'M SORRY. IT'S ALL MY F-F-F-F-F-FAULT.

OF COURSE, NONE OF THIS WOULD HAVE HAPPENED IF SHE'D JUST TOLD ME HER SECRET

HOWLLL

HA...SHE'S A STINKER.

DON'T WORRY -- THAT WOLF IS PROBABLY FAR AWAY...

HOWLLL

YOW!

SWACK

WHINNEY!

OOF!

PTUI.

OH, NO --

WHINNEY!

--NO, NO, NO!

COME BACK!

NO. NO.
NO. NO....
OOOO-KAY.

NO PROBLEM.
I CAN HANDLE
THIS --JUST PULL
MYSELF OUT
AND --

MMMPH!

WHUMPF!

PERFECT. JUST PERFECT.

SNOW, IT HAD TO BE SNOW, SHE COULDN'T HAVE HAD TR-TR-TROPICAL MAGIC...

AND COVER THE F-F-FJORDS WITH WHITE SANDS AND WARM --

FIRE!

ANNA HAS SPOTTED SMOKE IN THE DISTANCE. BUT AS SHE MOVES TOWARD IT...

...SHE SLIPS ON SOME ICE...

WHUP-WHUP-WHOA!

...ROLLS DOWN A HILL...

AAAAAAHHHHH--

...AND LANDS RIGHT IN A CHILLY STREAM.

ACK!

Kr·splash

COLD, COLD, COLD, COLD, COLD...

BUT AT LEAST IT GOT HER CLOSER TO THE FIRE.

...COLD, COLD, COLD, COLD...

...COLD, COLD -- LOOKS LIKE SOMEONE'S HOME. BUT WHO WOULD BE LIVING ALL ALONE OUT HERE?

MAYBE IF I BRUSH OFF SOME OF THIS SNOW...

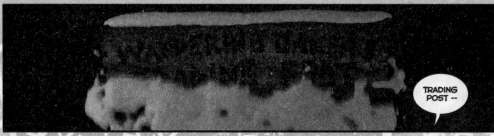

TRADING POST --

OH -- GREAT. FOR NOW, HOW ABOUT WINTER BOOTS...AND DRESSES?

THAT WOULD BE IN OUR WINTER DEPARTMENT.

...OH.

UM... I WAS JUST WONDERING -- HAS ANOTHER YOUNG WOMAN, THE QUEEN PERHAPS, I DON'T KNOW, PASSED THROUGH HERE?

ONLY ONE CRAZY ENOUGH TO BE OUT IN THIS STORM IS YOU, DEAR.

WHOOOSH!

ARE YOU OPEN FOR BUSINESS?

YOU AND THIS FELLOW....

UHH...

HOO HOO. BIG SUMMER BLOW OUT!

CARROTS.

...HUH...?

BEHIND YOU.

OH, RIGHT. EXCUSE ME.

OOH, THAT'S A ROUGH BUSINESS TO BE IN RIGHT NOW. I MEAN, THAT IS REALLY...

AHEM. THAT'S UNFORTUNATE.

STILL FORTY. BUT I WILL THROW IN A VISIT TO OAKEN'S SAUNA. HOO HOO! HI, FAMILY.

HOO HOO!

TEN'S ALL I GOT.

HELP ME OUT.

OKAY.

TEN WILL GET YOU THIS AND NO MORE.

OKAY. OKAY, I'M— OW!

BYE BYE.

WHOA!

FOR THE FIRST TIME SINCE THE FREAK STORM STARTED, KRISTOFF FOUND HIMSELF HAPPY FOR THE SNOW—

WHUMPF!

—IF NOTHING ELSE, IT MADE FOR A SOFT LANDING.

SNORT!

SNIFF SNIFF

SNRRRT?

...OH WELL, IT WAS ALL MY FAULT.

I GOT ENGAGED BUT THEN SHE FREAKED OUT BECAUSE I'D ONLY JUST MET HIM--

-- YOU KNOW, THAT DAY. AND SHE SAID SHE WOULDN'T BLESS THE MARRIAGE--

WAIT. YOU GOT ENGAGED TO SOMEONE YOU JUST MET?

YEAH. ANYWAY, I GOT MAD AND SO SHE GOT MAD AND THEN SHE TRIED TO WALK AWAY, AND I GRABBED HER GLOVE--

HANG ON. YOU MEAN TO TELL ME YOU GOT ENGAGED TO SOMEONE YOU JUST MET?!

YES. PAY ATTENTION.

BUT THE THING IS SHE WORE THE GLOVES ALL THE TIME...

...SO I JUST THOUGHT, MAYBE SHE HAS A THING ABOUT DIRT.

DIDN'T YOUR PARENTS EVER WARN YOU ABOUT STRANGERS?

YES, THEY DID.... BUT HANS IS NOT A STRANGER.

OH YEAH? WHAT'S HIS LAST NAME?

...OF-THE-SOUTHERN-ISLES?

WHAT'S HIS FAVORITE FOOD?

...SANDWICHES.

142

BUT THEN, SHE HEARS IT.

GRRRRRRRRRRRRRRRRRR

SVEN - GO.

GO!

WHAT ARE THEY?

WOLVES...

WOLVES?!

146

ANNA LOOKS FOR A WAY TO HELP KRISTOFF... AND FINDS ONE.

USING HER TORCH, SHE LIGHTS HIS BEDROLL ON FIRE...

KRISTOFF PULLS HIMSELF BACK ONTO THE SLED JUST IN TIME --

SNRRRT??!

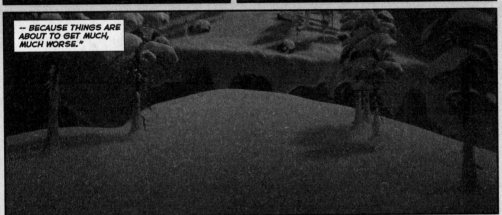

-- BECAUSE THINGS ARE ABOUT TO GET MUCH, MUCH WORSE."

OH!

GET READY TO JUMP, SVEN!

YOU DON'T TELL HIM WHAT TO DO - I DO!

ANNA WAS ABOUT TO PROTEST WHEN KRISTOFF SCOOPED HER UP AND TOSSED HER ONTO SVEN'S BACK...

--OOF!

OKAY, NOW--

SVISH

...AND THEN CUT THE ROPES THAT HELD SVEN TO THE SLED.

JUMP, SVEN!

JUMP!

AAAAGGHHH!!!

AAAAAGGGHHH!!!

AWRRHR!

SVEN CLEARS THE GORGE WITHOUT ANY TROUBLE --

OOOF!

--BUT THE SLED DOESN'T HAVE ENOUGH SPEED TO CROSS THE GAP.

KRISTOFF JUMPS AT THE LAST SECOND...

YES!

GRRRRR

GRRRRR

GRRRRR

WHEW.

HANGING ON THE EDGE, KRISTOFF TAKES A QUICK LOOK BELOW FOR HIS SLED.

MAYBE THE SNOW BROKE ITS FALL?

WHOOM!

AW -- BUT I JUST PAID IT OFF --!

UH-OH. NO, NO, NO

SWOOSH!

HANG ON!

AS ANNA SETS OFF ON HER OWN, KRISTOFF AND SVEN WEIGH THEIR OPTIONS.

SNRRT?

OF COURSE I DON'T WANT TO HELP HER ANYMORE. IN FACT, THIS WHOLE THING HAS RUINED ME FOR HELPING ANYONE EVER AGAIN.

but she'll die on her own.

I CAN LIVE WITH THAT.

but you won't get your new sled if she's dead.

...YOU KNOW SOMETIMES I REALLY DON'T LIKE YOU.

SIGH HOLD UP! WE'RE COMING!

YOU ARE?!

I MEAN -- SURE, I'LL LET YOU TAG ALONG.

...

LATER... ANNA AND KRISTOFF CONTINUE UP THE MOUNTAIN.

PAUSING TO CATCH HER BREATH, ANNA LOOKS DOWN TO SEE...

GASP

ARENDELLE.

IT'S COMPLETELY FROZEN.

...BUT IT'LL BE FINE. ELSA WILL THAW IT.

WILL SHE?

...YEAH. NOW COME ON. THIS WAY TO THE NORTH MOUNTAIN?

MORE LIKE THIS WAY.

OH...

EVERY SUMMER, THE VALLEY AT THE BASE OF THE MOUNTAIN IS FILLED WITH FLOWERS AND BIRDS SINGING IN THE WARM SUNSHINE...

...ALMOST EVERY SUMMER...

I NEVER KNEW WINTER COULD BE SO BEAUTIFUL.

YEAH... IT REALLY IS BEAUTIFUL, ISN'T IT?

BUT IT'S SO WHITE, YOU KNOW?

??

??

HOW ABOUT A LITTLE COLOR?

I'M THINKING, LIKE, MAYBE SOME CRIMSON...

...OR CHARTREUSE...

HOW 'BOUT YELLOW....

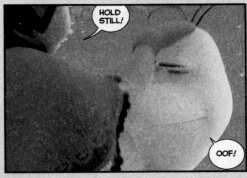

WELL... ALMOST...

IT WAS LIKE MY WHOLE LIFE GOT TURNED UPSIDE DOWN.

HERE --

OOF!

FOONF

OUCH.

OH! TOO HARD. I'M SORRY. I - I - I WAS JUST...

HEAD RUSH!

ARE YOU OKAY?

ARE YOU KIDDING ME?

I - AM WONDERFUL!

I'VE WANTED A NOSE!

SO CUTE. IT'S LIKE A LITTLE BABY UNICORN.

I CAN FIX THIS --!

WHACK!

OOH!

WHAT? HEY! WHOA!

OH, I LOVE IT EVEN MORE! HAH... ALL RIGHT...

...LET'S START THIS THING OVER.

HI EVERYONE. I'M OLAF. AND I LIKE WARM HUGS.

OLAF...?

...THAT'S RIGHT, OLAF.

DO YOU THINK YOU COULD SHOW US THE WAY?

...HOW DOES THIS WORK --?

WHACK!

STOP IT, SVEN. TRYING TO FOCUS HERE.

YEAH, WHY?

I'LL TELL YOU WHY. WE NEED ELSA TO BRING BACK SUMMER.

SUMMER!!

OH, I DON'T KNOW WHY BUT I'VE ALWAYS LOVED THE IDEA OF SUMMER, AND SUN, AND ALL THINGS HOT.

REALLY? I'M GUESSING YOU DON'T HAVE MUCH EXPERIENCE WITH HEAT.

NOPE. BUT SOMETIMES I LIKE TO CLOSE MY EYES...

"...BECAUSE THEN I'M HEADING TO THE BEACH.

OH! I COULD GET A TAN! I'VE ALWAYS WANTED A TAN.

IT'D BE A GREAT LOOK FOR ME.

OHHHH, YEAH.

"AND THEN THERE'S SAILING...

"...WHICH WOULD BE SO MUCH EASIER ON UNFROZEN WAVES!

"AND SO WOULD SWIMMING!

WHEE

WHO KNEW I'D BE SO GREAT AT FLOATING?

"THEN I'LL GET BACK TO THE SHORE AND SEE...

"ALL OF MY FRIENDS, JUST WAITING FOR ME.

CAN I BORROW YOUR HAT?

IT'LL BE A COOL TIME ON A WARM DAY--

WHEN I FINALLY SEE SUMMER...!

FULL OF DANCING AND PLAYING ON THE BOARDWALK!

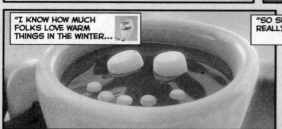

"I KNOW HOW MUCH FOLKS LOVE WARM THINGS IN THE WINTER...

"SO SUMMER MUST REALLY BE GREAT!

IT'LL BE SO WONDERFUL ...

WHEN I FINALLY GET TO EXPERIENCE MY VERY FIRST HOT, SUNNY DAY...

WHEN THAT DAY COMES, I'M GOING TO BE...

YOU CAN BE THERE TO SEE THE LOOK ON MY FACE...

WHEN I FINALLY FIND MY WAY INTO SUMMER!

HE DOESN'T KNOW, DOES HE? I GOTTA TELL HIM.

DON'T EVEN THINK ABOUT IT.

IT'S WHAT I DREAM OF --

--SOME DAY I'LL SEE IT!

THE GREEN! THE WARM! I'M READY-

-- FOR SUMMER!

SO COME ON! ELSA'S THIS WAY.

LET'S GO BRING BACK SUMMER!

HAHA! OKAY, I'M COMING!

SOMEBODY HAS REALLY GOT TO TELL HIM.

THE MAGICAL WINTER CONTINUES TO HOLD ARENDELLE IN ITS ICY GRIP, AND THE TEMPERS OF ITS CITIZENS ARE STARTING TO RUN HOT.

WHEN FIREWOOD GETS WET, IT WON'T CATCH FIRE. THAT'S WHY YOU STACK IT BARK UP.

BARK DOWN IS DRIER. EVERYBODY KNOWS THAT.

PRINCESS ANNA IS IN TROUBLE.

I NEED VOLUNTEERS TO GO WITH ME TO FIND HER!

I'LL GO!

I VOLUNTEER!

I VOLUNTEER TWO MEN, MY LORD!

BE PREPARED FOR ANYTHING. AND SHOULD YOU ENCOUNTER THE QUEEN...

...YOU ARE TO PUT AN END TO THIS WINTER, DO YOU UNDERSTAND?

SO HOW EXACTLY ARE YOU PLANNING TO STOP THIS WEATHER?

I'M GONNA TALK TO MY SISTER.

THAT'S YOUR PLAN? YOU MEAN MY ICE BUSINESS IS RIDING ON YOU...TALKING TO YOUR SISTER?

YUP.

SO YOU'RE NOT AT ALL...

...AFRAID OF HER?

NO. WHY WOULD I BE?

YEAH, I BET ELSA'S THE NICEST, GENTLEST...

...WARMEST PERSON EVER.

OH, LOOK AT THAT. I'VE BEEN IMPALED.

HAHAHA!

SEVERAL HOURS SPENT TRUDGING THROUGH THE SNOW LATER...

SO WHAT NOW?

I HAVE NO IDEA. IT'S TOO STEEP TO HIKE UP.

I'VE ONLY GOT ONE ROPE, AND YOU DON'T KNOW HOW TO CLIMB MOUNTAINS.

SAYS YOU.

UM..., WHAT ARE YOU DOING?

...PLEASE TELL ME I'M ALMOST THERE.

NOT QUITE...

DOES THE AIR *PUFF* SEEM A BIT THIN UP HERE TO YOU?

JUST HANG ON--

HEY, SVEN?

NOT SURE IF THIS IS GOING TO SOLVE THE PROBLEM, BUT I FOUND A STAIRCASE THAT LEADS EXACTLY WHERE YOU WANT TO GO

HA HA! THANK GOODNESS!

CATCH!

OOOF!

THANKS!

THAT WAS LIKE A CRAZY TRUST EXERCISE.

THE STAIRS LEAD STRAIGHT UP THE MOUNTAIN.

AND AT THE TOP...

...ELSA'S ICE PALACE.

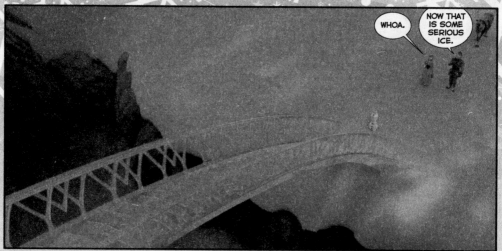

WHOA.

NOW THAT IS SOME SERIOUS ICE.

I THINK I MIGHT CRY.

GO AHEAD. I WON'T JUDGE. COME ON, OLAF.

I DON'T THINK THAT'S A GOOD IDEA, SVEN...

KLOP   KLOP

SLIP

WHUMP!

TAKE IT EASY. I GOTCHA.

YOU STAY RIGHT HERE, BUDDY.

I JUST CAN'T GET OVER THIS ICE. FLAWLESS.

OKAY. KNOCK.

JUST... KNOCK.

WHY ISN'T SHE KNOCKING? DO YOU THINK SHE KNOWS HOW TO KNOCK?

THE SOUND OF ANNA'S KNOCK ECHOES THROUGHOUT THE PALACE AS THE DOOR SLOWLY BEGINS TO OPEN.

HA. IT OPENED. THAT'S A FIRST.

UM... YOU SHOULD PROBABLY WAIT OUT HERE.

WHAT?!

WELL, IT'S JUST, LAST TIME I INTRODUCED ELSA TO A GUY, SHE FROZE EVERYTHING.

BUT IT'S A PALACE MADE OF ICE. ICE IS MY LIFE!

BYE, SVEN.

YOU TOO, OLAF.

ME?

JUST... GIVE US A MINUTE.

OKAY. ONE... TWO...

...THREE... FOUR....

ANNA GREW UP IN A CASTLE. IT WAS HUGE, WITH HUNDREDS OF ROOMS AND HALLWAYS THAT SEEMED TO GO ON FOREVER.

BUT NOW IT FELT PRACTICALLY TINY. HOW COULD HER SISTER HAVE MADE ALL THIS?

AND THE BEAUTY --
THE BEAUTY TOOK
HER BREATH AWAY.

ELSA?
IT'S ME...

THEN THE ECHO
ANSWERS BACK.

ANNA.

ANNA CAN HARDLY BELIEVE HER
EYES. HER SISTER LOOKS SO
BEAUTIFUL, SO CONFIDENT. LIKE
THIS IS WHAT SHE WAS ALWAYS
MEANT TO BE.

ELSA, YOU LOOK... DIFFERENT. IT'S A GOOD DIFFERENT, THOUGH. AND THIS PLACE IS AMAZING.

THANK YOU. I NEVER...I NEVER KNEW WHAT I WAS CAPABLE OF.

I'M SO SORRY ABOUT WHAT HAPPENED. IF I HAD KNOWN--

NO, IT'S OKAY. YOU DON'T HAVE TO APOLOGIZE...

BUT YOU SHOULD PROBABLY GO.

YOU BELONG IN ARENDELLE.

YOU BUILT ME. DO YOU REMEMBER THAT?

AND YOU'RE... ALIVE?

UM... I THINK SO.

HE'S JUST LIKE THE ONE WE BUILT AS KIDS. WE CAN BE CLOSE LIKE THAT AGAIN.

ELSA WANTS THAT TO BE TRUE MORE THAN ANYTHING.

ONLY SHE KNOWS WHAT WILL HAPPEN.

BECAUSE IT ALREADY HAPPENED ONCE BEFORE.

SHE DIDN'T MEAN TO.

BUT IT WAS STILL HER FAULT.

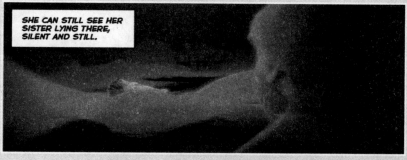

SHE CAN STILL SEE HER SISTER LYING THERE, SILENT AND STILL.

SHE CAN STILL FEEL HER SISTER'S SKIN, COLD AS ICE.

AND SHE DOESN'T EVER WANT THAT TO HAPPEN AGAIN. SHE DOESN'T EVER WANT TO FEEL THAT AGAIN.

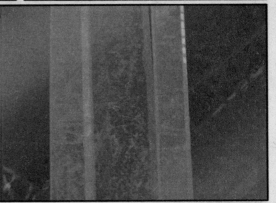

I UNDERSTAND; I DO.

AND I KNOW...

...IF YOU COME BACK...

...WE CAN FIX THIS.

TOGETHER.

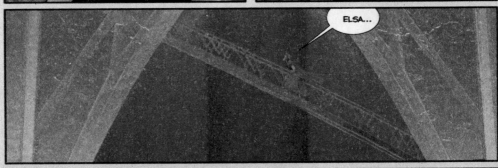

ELSA...

PLEASE COME HOME.

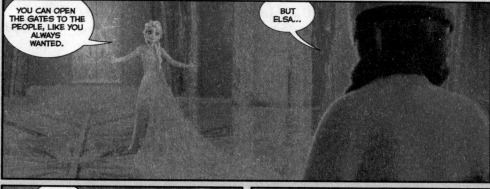

ANNA, I KNOW YOU MEAN WELL...

BUT YOU HAVE TO LEAVE ME BE.

I KNOW I'M ALONE... BUT I'M FINALLY FREE.

...NOW PLEASE, LEAVE ME HERE.

ANNA, YOU'RE NOT SAFE HERE!

YOU HAVE TO GO!

WE CAN DO THIS, ELSA, TOGETHER!

NO!

WE CAN FIX EVERYTHING!

IT'LL ALL BE --

I CAN'T!

UNGH!

...OH.

...UNH!

...ANNA?

GASP!

ANNA!

ARE YOU OKAY?

I'M OKAY. I'M FINE.

WHO IS THIS?

WAIT, IT DOESN'T MATTER -- JUST...

YOU HAVE TO GO.

NO. I KNOW WE CAN FIGURE THIS OUT TOGETHER!

HOW? WHAT POWER DO YOU HAVE TO STOP THIS WINTER? TO STOP ME?

ANNA, I THINK WE SHOULD GO.

NO. I'M NOT LEAVING WITHOUT YOU, ELSA!

YES, YOU ARE.

FWOOSH

RRRUMMMBLLLEE

WHAT A CUTE MARSHMALLOW SNOWMAN!

GASP!

HRRRRRRR

STOP! PUT US DOWN!

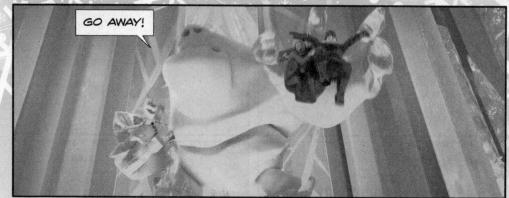

HEEEYAH!

OH, COME ON!

IT WAS JUST A LITTLE SNOWBALL ANNA THREW.

SPLAT

IT SHOULDN'T HAVE BOTHERED MARSHMALLOW AT ALL.

HRRRAAAAAGHHH!

OH, SEE? NOW YOU MADE HIM MAD!

I'LL DISTRACT HIM. YOU GUYS GO.

DOWN THE MOUNTAIN KRISTOFF AND ANNA GO, PICKING UP SPEED, BOTH THINKING THE SAME THING...

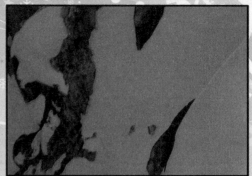

"WE HAVE TO OUTRUN THAT GIGANTIC MONSTER SNOWMAN."

HRRRAAAAAGHH!

WHAM

RUN!

THEY RUN FOR ALL THEY'RE WORTH...

...WITH MARSHMALLOW FOLLOWING CLOSE BEHIND, AND GETTING CLOSER.

THEY NEED A PLAN... AND ANNA COMES UP WITH ONE.

WHAT ARE YOU DOING WITH THAT TREE??

WATCH!

SPLA-BLAAAMM!

GOT HIM! HAHAHA!

OKAY...

WHAT IF WE FALL?

THERE'S TWENTY FEET OF FRESH POWDER DOWN THERE --

IT'LL BE LIKE LANDING ON A PILLOW.

HOPEFULLY.

TOOM TOOMTOOM

HHHRRRRROOOOOOAAAAAAARRRRRR

OK, ANNA. ON THREE.

ONE...

OKAY. YOU TELL ME WHEN...

"I'M READY TO GO."

I WAS BORN READY! YES!

CALM DOWN.

TWO...

TREE!!

SHPHLOOSHH

WHAT THE--

WHOA!!

SKRICH

OOF!

...THAT HAPPENED.

AH.

AH.

MAN, I AM OUT OF SHAPE.

THERE WE GO.

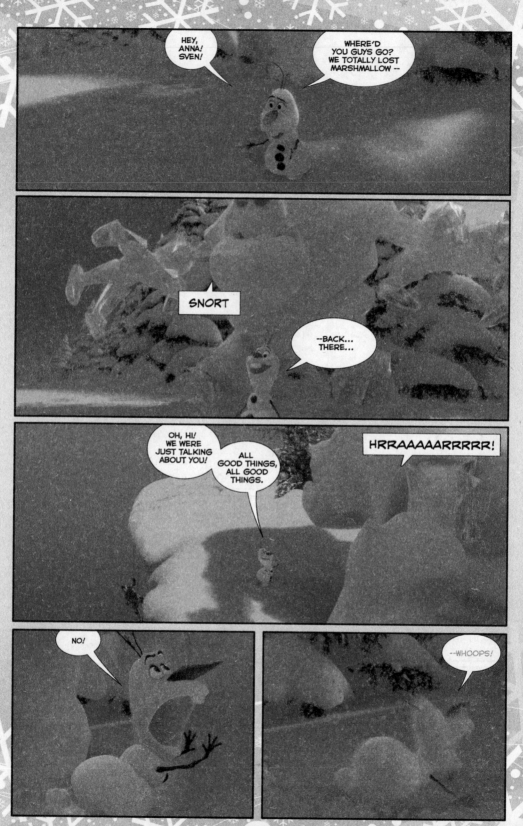

HANG IN THERE, GUYS!

YOINK

WAIT, WHAT?

WHAT'S HAPPENING?

KRISTOFF DIDN'T NEED TO ANSWER... THEY COULD BOTH SEE MARSHMALLOW HAULING THEM BACK UP THE MOUNTAIN.

...AND NOT GENTLY.

BONK!

AAAOOOWWW!

KRISTOFF!!

GRRAAARRR!

DON'T COME BACK!

...

WE... WE WON'T.

BEFORE MARSHMALLOW CAN DO ANYTHING ELSE, ANNA SLICES THE ROPE WITH A SMALL KNIFE.

WHOOOAAAAAAAAA----!!

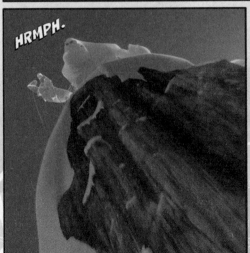

HRMPH.

--AAAAAAAAAAAAAA--

FOOMF

HA. IT'S FINE.

I'VE GOT A THICK SKULL.

I DON'T HAVE A SKULL.

...OR BONES.

...SO.

NOW WHAT?

NOW WHAT?

NOW WHAT?! OH!

WHAT AM I GONNA DO? SHE THREW ME OUT. I CAN'T GO BACK TO ARENDELLE WITH THE WEATHER LIKE THIS.

AND THEN THERE'S YOUR ICE BUSINESS--

HEY, DON'T WORRY ABOUT MY ICE BUSINESS... WORRY ABOUT-- YOUR HAIR?!?

WHAT? I JUST FELL OFF A CLIFF. YOU SHOULD SEE YOUR HAIR.

NO, YOURS IS TURNING WHITE.

WHITE? IT'S WHAT?

DOES IT LOOK BAD?

...

NO.

YOU HESITATED.

NO, I DIDN'T.

ANNA, YOU NEED HELP. NOW COME ON.

OKAY! WHERE ARE WE GOING?

TO SEE MY FRIENDS.

THE LOVE EXPERTS?

DON'T...

POP!

CRAK!

A CREAKING AND CRACKLING INTERRUPTS ELSA.

CRAKLE

CRAK!

IT GROWS LOUDER, AND WHEN IT IS DONE...

...THERE IS MORE ICE THAN EVER.

MEANWHILE, IN THE MOUNTAINS.

LOOK, SVEN...

THE SKY'S AWAKE.

HFF HFF

ARE YOU COLD?

...THEY'RE ROCKS.

HEY GUYS!

HE'S CRAZY.

WOW, I DIDN'T EVEN RECOGNIZE YOU, YOU'VE LOST SO MUCH WEIGHT!

I'LL DISTRACT HIM WHILE YOU RUN.

HI, SVEN'S FAMILY! IT'S NICE TO MEET YOU!

ANNA, BECAUSE I LOVE YOU, I INSIST YOU RUN.

I UNDERSTAND YOU'RE LOVE EXPERTS!

WHY AREN'T YOU RUNNING?

UM...

225

UM, OKAY, WELL... I'M GONNA GO--

JUST THEN, THE ROCKS BEGIN ROLLING TOWARDS KRISTOFF.

NO NO NO, ANNA -WAIT!

rumblerumblerumble

KRISTOFF!

rumblerumblerumble

OH!

rumblerumblerumble

OOOH!

rumblerumblerumble

rumblerumblerumble

rumblerumblerumble

KRISTOFF'S HOME!

IT'S BEEN TOO LONG!

KRISTOFF'S HOME!

WAIT -- WHO IS KRISTOFF?

KRISTOFF, PICK ME UP!

OOF! YOU'RE GETTING BIG! GOOD FOR YOU!

TROLLS?

PICK ME UP, TOO!

HE BROUGHT A GIRL?

HE BROUGHT A GIRL?

HE BROUGHT A GIRL?

HE BROUGHT A GIRL?

HE BROUGHT A GIRL?

HE BROUGHT A GIRL?

AND I'D CALL THAT A SIGN!

YOU'RE BOTH A BIT OFF-KILTER — YOU TWO WERE CLEARLY MEANT FOR EACH OTHER!

WHEN PEOPLE ARE ANGRY OR SCARED, THEY CAN MAKE BAD DECISIONS...

BUT LOVE? THAT CAN BRING OUT THE BEST IN THEM.

WOW.

AND I THINK YOU TWO WILL BRING OUT THE BEST IN EACH OTHER!

WE ALL NEED TO FIND PEOPLE WE CAN LOVE.

FAMILY... FRIENDS... THEY MAKE LIFE BETTER.

THEY MAKE US BETTER!

237

239

THE NEXT MORNING, AT ELSA'S PALACE.

WE ARE HERE TO FIND PRINCESS ANNA.

BE ON GUARD, BUT NO HARM IS TO COME TO THE QUEEN.

DO YOU UNDERSTAND?

YES, PRINCE HANS.

HRRAAAAARRRRR!

GO AWAY!

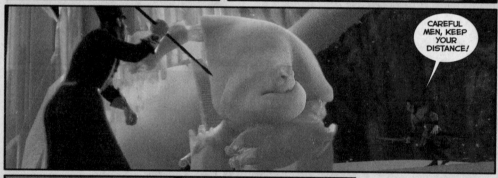

CAREFUL MEN, KEEP YOUR DISTANCE!

AS PRINCE HANS FACES MARSHMALLOW...

THE DUKE'S THUGS CHARGE UP THE STAIRS...

GO! GO!

COME ON!

...AND PURSUE ELSA TO THE TOP FLOOR OF HER PALACE.

WATCH YOUR BACK --
NO TELLING WHAT
HORRORS SHE HAS
IN THIS ICY
TOWER!

SHE'S UP
THERE -
COME ON!

246

FOR A SPLIT SECOND, ELSA STARES AT THE ARROW, TRAPPED IN ICE AND REALIZES.

SHE'S NOT HELPLESS.

FWOOSH

CRAKCRAKCRAK.

SHE CAN DEFEND HERSELF.

STAY AWAY!

GET HER! GET HER!

GO 'ROUND -- I HAVE HER COVERED HERE!

FWOOSH

CRAKCRAKCRAK

MEANWHILE, OUTSIDE THE ICE PALACE...

HRRAAAAARRRRR!

...PRINCE HANS BARELY DODGES THE CREATURE'S FOOT.

WHAM

GASP

HELP HIM UP!

MEANWHILE, IN THE PALACE...

TAKE AIM...

...ELSA IS SURROUNDED.

WITH A PUSH OF HER POWER...

CREEEEAK

CRAKCRAKCRAK

GASP

CRACK

STOP MOVING! YOU'LL ONLY HURT YOURSELF!

AS ELSA CONCENTRATES ON THE FIRST GUARD...

...SHE FINDS HERSELF IN THE SIGHTS OF AN EVEN GREATER DANGER...!

FWOOSH

CRAKCRACKCRAK

SUDDENLY...

CRAKCRACKCRAK

...ELSA PUSHES HIM AWAY WITH A WALL OF ICE.

FWOOSH

CRAKCRACKCRAK

CRAKCRA
CRAKCRA

NO--

ELSA'S MAGIC PUSHES HARDER...

FWOOSH

UGH--

CRAKCRA
CRAKCRA

...UNTIL THE DUKE'S GUARD IS PUSHED RIGHT THROUGH THE ICE PALACE'S OUTER WALL.

KR-KRASHHH

AND THEN, SHE PUSHES FURTHER.

CRAKCRA
CRAKCRA

SKRRREEEEE

NFFF--

HF
HF

CRAKCRA
CRAKCRAK-K-K

QUEEN ELSA!

QUEEN ELSA. PLEASE.

CRAKCRA CRAKCRA

...DON'T BE THE MONSTER THEY FEAR YOU ARE.

...

FWOOSH

CRAKCRA
CRAKCRA

HANS' WORDS REACH ELSA, AND
SHE STOPS. SHE DIDN'T REALLY
WANT TO HURT THE GUARDS...

...BUT THEY STILL
WANT TO HURT HER.

NO -- !

WHILE HANS IS ABLE TO KNOCK THE CROSSBOW'S AIM OFF...

...THE BOLT FIRES, NOT AT ELSA, BUT UP...

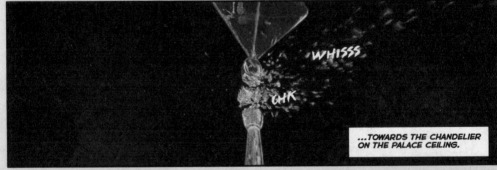

WHISSS

CHK

...TOWARDS THE CHANDELIER ON THE PALACE CEILING.

OH!

ELSA AWAKENS, SLOWLY, BY THE LIGHT OF A WINDOW IN THE ARENDELLE CASTLE DUNGEON...

AND SHE LOOKS TO SEE WHAT SHE HAS DONE TO ARENDELLE.

KR-CHANK

262

JUST HANG IN THERE...

C'MON, BUDDY!

FASTER!

SNORT

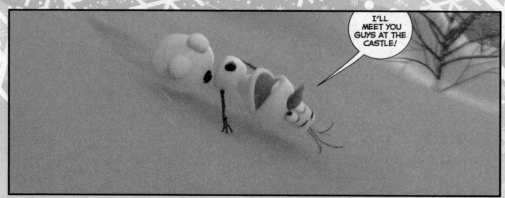

IT'S PRINCESS ANNA!

I'VE GOT YOU.

...ARE YOU G-GONNA BE OKAY?

DON'T WORRY ABOUT ME.

ANNA! OH, YOU HAD US WORRIED SICK!

MY LADY, YOU ARE FREEZING.

YOU POOR GIRL... LET'S GET YOU INSIDE.

GET HER WARM AND FIND PRINCE HANS, IMMEDIATELY.

WE WILL.

THANK YOU.

MAKE SURE SHE'S SAFE!

SLAM

SIGH.

HANS,
NO...

STOP

BUT THEN
SHE DOOMED
HERSELF--

--AND
YOU WERE DUMB
ENOUGH TO
GO AFTER
HER!

IT'S GETTING COLDER BY THE MINUTE. IF WE DON'T DO SOMETHING SOON, WE'LL ALL FREEZE TO DEATH.

PRINCE HANS!

PRINCESS ANNA... IS DEAD.

WHAT?

NO!

MON DIEU!

WHAT HAPPENED TO HER?

SHE WAS KILLED...

...BY QUEEN ELSA.

HER OWN SISTER!

AT LEAST WE GOT TO SAY OUR MARRIAGE VOWS... BEFORE SHE DIED IN MY ARMS.

THERE CAN BE NO DOUBT NOW; QUEEN ELSA IS A MONSTER AND WE ARE ALL IN GRAVE DANGER.

PRINCE HANS, ARENDELLE LOOKS TO YOU.

WITH A HEAVY HEART, I CHARGE QUEEN ELSA OF ARENDELLE WITH TREASON...

...AND SENTENCE HER TO DEATH.

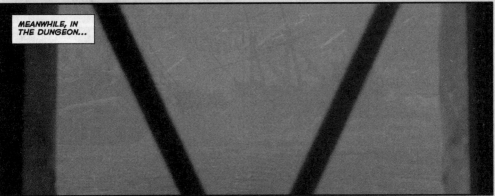

MEANWHILE, IN THE DUNGEON...

OH!

CRAKCRACK CRAKCRACK

CRAKCRACK
CRAKCRACK

NFFF!

CRAKCRACK

HURRY UP!

SHE'S DANGEROUS.

MOVE QUICKLY!

BECAUSE ELSA HAS ESCAPED.

AWWWF

SNORT

I DON'T UNDERSTAND YOU WHEN YOU TALK LIKE THAT.

AAAH!

STOP IT! PUT ME DOWN!

PFFFT.

BRAWW!

NO, SVEN, WE ARE NOT GOING BACK.

--SHE'S WITH HER TRUE LOVE.

SIGH

WHAT THE --

ANNA!

SNRRT!

GO!

287

EEP!

AHH, THERE WE GO.

SKRITCH

O-OLAF?

WOOOOW.

OLAF, GET AWAY FROM THERE!

SO THIS IS HEAT. I LOVE IT.

OH! BUT DON'T TOUCH IT!

COME ON -- LET'S GET YOU WARMED UP.

SO, WHERE'S HANS? WHAT HAPPENED TO YOUR KISS?

I WAS WRONG ABOUT HIM. IT WASN'T TRUE LOVE.

BUT WE RAN ALL THE WAY HERE!

PLEASE, OLAF. YOU C-CAN'T STAY HERE. YOU'LL MELT.

I AM NOT LEAVING HERE UNTIL WE FIND SOME OTHER ACT OF TRUE LOVE TO SAVE YOU.

...DO YOU HAPPEN TO HAVE ANY IDEAS?

I DON'T EVEN KNOW WHAT LOVE IS.

SOME PEOPLE ARE WORTH MELTING FOR...

...BUT MAYBE NOT THIS SECOND!

KRAK

DON'T WORRY, I'VE GOT IT!

NFF

WE'RE GONNA GET THROUGH--

293

OH, WAIT.

HANG ON, I'M GETTING SOMETHING...

Krak

CRUNCH

AH! IT'S KRISTOFF AND SVEN!

THEY'RE COMING BACK THIS WAY!

THEY-THEY ARE?

WOW, HE'S REALLY MOVING FAST. I GUESS I WAS WRONG.

I GUESS KRISTOFF DOESN'T LOVE YOU ENOUGH TO LEAVE YOU BEHIND.

HELP ME UP, OLAF! PLEASE!

NO-NO-NO-NO-NO!

STAY BY THE FIRE AND KEEP WARM!

I NEED TO GET TO KRISTOFF.

WHY?

OH! OH I KNOW WHY!

THERE'S YOUR ACT OF TRUE LOVE RIGHT THERE, RIDING ACROSS THE FJORDS LIKE A VALIANT, PUNGENT REINDEER KING! COME ON!

OH, GULP!

CRAKCRACK
CRAKCRACK

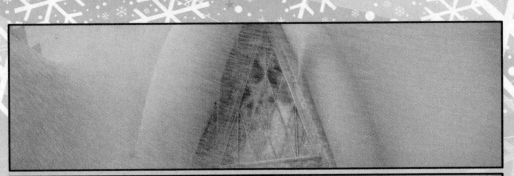

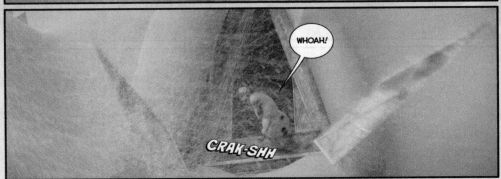

WHOAH!

CRAK-SHH

THE STORM IS OUT OF CONTROL!

SLIDE, ANNA!

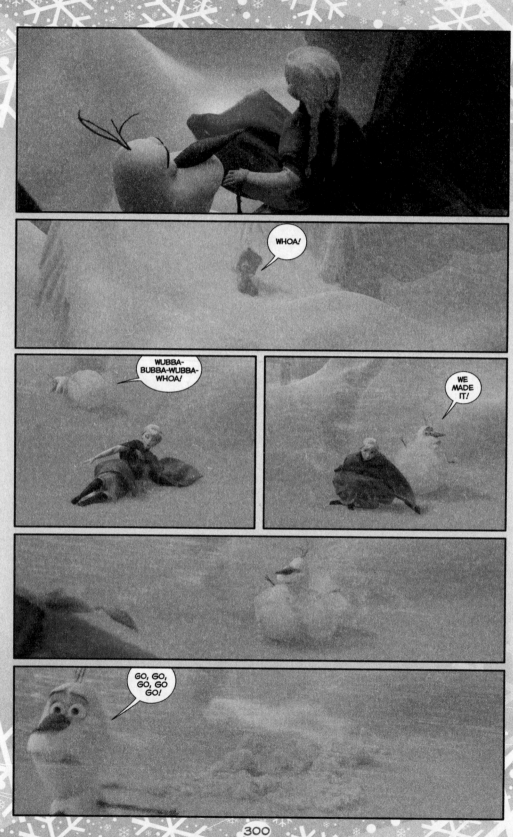

KRISTOFF RACES ONTO THE FROZEN FJORDS, TOWARDS ANNA...

...NOT KNOWING THAT, SOMEWHERE IN THE APPROACHING WINDSTORM, SHE'S LOOKING FOR HIM.

BRR--

C'MON, BUDDY - FASTER!

BRAAW!

KRISTOFF...?

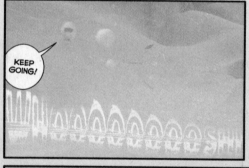

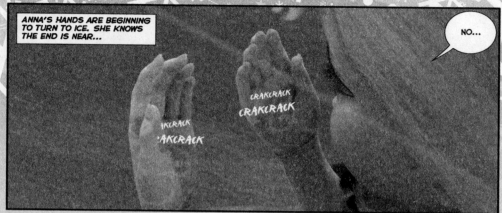

ANNA'S HANDS ARE BEGINNING TO TURN TO ICE. SHE KNOWS THE END IS NEAR...

NO...

CRAKCRACK
CRAKCRACK

'AKCRACK
'AKCRACK

HER HEART IS BEGINNING TO FREEZE.

THE SHIP --

IT'S COMING APART!

GO!

JUST -- JUST TAKE CARE OF MY SISTER!

YOUR SISTER? SHE RETURNED FROM THE MOUNTAIN WEAK AND COLD. SHE SAID YOU FROZE HER HEART!

WHAT? NO!

I TRIED TO SAVE HER, BUT IT WAS TOO LATE. HER SKIN WAS ICE, HER HAIR TURNED WHITE...

YOUR SISTER IS DEAD...

...BECAUSE OF YOU.

ELSA IS STUNNED. THE SHOCK OF ANNA'S DEATH CAUSES THE SWIRLING STORM TO FREEZE, SNOWFLAKES SUSPENDED IN MID-AIR, TRAPPED IN GRIEF.

K-K-

KRISTOFF?

ANNA.

...KRISTOFF...

ANNA!

THE SOUND OF A SWORD BEING DRAWN CAUSES ANNA'S HEAD TO TURN.

SHIIIIING

ANNA CAN FEEL HER HEART SLOWING, TURNING TO ICE.

SHE COULD RUN TO KRISTOFF AND BE SAVED BY A TRUE LOVE'S KISS...

...OR SHE COULD HELP HER SISTER. THERE'S NOT TIME TO DO BOTH.

...ANNA?

NO!

IT IS THE LAST THING ANNA DOES...

CRAKCRACK

...BEFORE THE REST OF HER BODY TRANSFORMS INTO ICE.

CRAKCRACKKKK

SHRKRAAAKKLLKRAK

WHAT?!?

HANS SHOULD HAVE EASILY CUT THROUGH THE ICE STATUE ANNA HAD BECOME...

...BUT THE SAME MAGIC THAT HAS FROZEN HER INSTEAD SHATTERS HIS BLADE... AND SENDS HIM FLYING.

CRAKCRACKRRR

ANNA?

...OH.

WITH THE STORM FROZEN IN PLACE, EVERYONE HAD A CLEAR VIEW OF WHAT HAD HAPPENED.

HOW HANS HAD LIED ABOUT ANNA...

...AND HOW ANNA HAD HEROICALLY SAVED HER SISTER.

AND THEN, WHILE QUEEN ELSA SOBBED, THEY SAW SOMETHING ELSE...

KRICKLE

KRICKLE

GASP

SNRTT?

KRICKLEKRI
CKLEKRICK

OH!

...THEY SAW THE POWER OF TRUE LOVE.

I LOVE YOU.

AH! AN ACT OF TRUE LOVE WILL THAW A FROZEN HEART!

LOVE WILL THAW.

LOVE, OF COURSE!

ELSA?

LOVE!

SNRRTT?

THE FROZEN FJORD THAWS.

OH!

LOOK!

ICED OVER FOUNTAINS SPRING BACK TO LIFE.

THE SNOW LIFTS...

...SWEEPING UP ALL OF THE ICE ELSA HAD CREATED.

FLOWERS BLOOM.

HEE HEE!

THE SKY CLEARS.

THE SNOW SWIRLS...

...AND RISES...

...AND DISAPPEARS.

SHE HAS FINALLY SOLVED THE PUZZLE.

FREE OF THE FEARS OF HER CHILDHOOD, THE KEY TO CONTROLLING HER POWER WAS LOVE.

ANNA'S LOVE SHOWED HER THE WAY.

OH!

I KNEW YOU COULD DO IT!

AHEM.

ANNA?

BUT SHE FROZE YOUR HEART!

THE ONLY FROZEN HEART AROUND HERE --

-- IS YOURS.

WHAM

OW--

YAAAAAAHH--

SPLURRSHH

HAHAHAHA!

FANTASTIQUE!

HAHAHAHA!

BRRAAAW.

A FEW DAYS LATER...

I WILL RETURN THIS SCOUNDREL, HANS, TO HIS COUNTRY.

WE WILL SEE WHAT HIS TWELVE BIG BROTHERS THINK OF HIS BEHAVIOR.

ARENDELLE THANKS YOU, MY LORD.

THIS IS UNACCEPTABLE. I AM INNOCENT. I'M A VICTIM OF FEAR, I'VE BEEN TRAUMATIZED.

OW! MY NECK HURTS! IS THERE A DOCTOR I COULD...

...NO?

AND I DEMAND TO SEE THE QUEEN!

OH, I HAVE A MESSAGE FROM THE QUEEN.

ARENDELLE WILL HENCEFORTH AND FOREVER NO LONGER DO BUSINESS OF ANY SORT WITH WEASELTOWN.

WESELTON.

IT'S WESELTON!

MEANWHILE...

COME ON! C'MON, C'MON, C'MON!

OKAY, OKAY, HERE I COME--

OW! -- POLE.

WHUNG

OOPS. SORRY.

YOU HAVE TO. NO RETURNS. NO EXCHANGES. QUEEN'S ORDERS.

SNRRT.

SHE'S NAMED YOU THE OFFICIAL ARENDELLE ICE MASTER AND DELIVERER.

IT EVEN HAS A CUP HOLDER!

--DO YOU LIKE IT?

LIKE IT? I LOVE IT! I COULD KISS YOU!

...I COULD. I MEAN I'D LIKE TO. I'D... MAY I? WE ME....I MEAN, MAY WE?

THANKS, SVEN!

ARE YOU READY?

CLAP CLAP CLAP CLAP CLAP CLAP

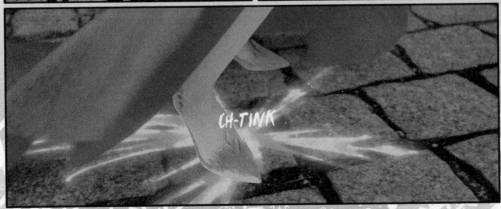

CH-TINK

ELSA LETS LOOSE HER MAGIC AGAIN, IN FULL CONTROL, AND WITH NO FEAR...

WOO!

WOO!

HER PEOPLE HAVE ACCEPTED HER, NOT AS A QUEEN WITH A CURSE --

CRAKCRACK

CRAKCRACK

-- BUT A QUEEN WITH A WONDERFUL GIFT.

HAHA!

WHEE!

WHOAH-OOOP.

I LIKE THE OPEN GATES.

HA-HAH! HEY, GUYS!

THAT'S RIGHT, ANNA-GLIDE AND PIVOT.

GLIDE AND PIVOT...

LAUGHTER RINGS OUT INTO THE NIGHT AS THE WHOLE VILLAGE HAS FUN.

AND ALL IS RIGHT IN ARENDELLE.

THE END.

DIRECTED BY
CHRIS BUCK
JENNIFER LEE

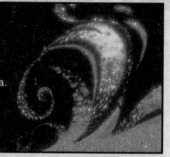

PRODUCED BY
PETER DEL VECHO, p.g.a.

EXECUTIVE PRODUCER
JOHN LASSETER

SCREENPLAY BY
JENNIFER LEE

STORY INSPIRED BY
"THE SNOW QUEEN"
BY HANS CHRISTIAN ANDERSEN

STORY BY
CHRIS BUCK
JENNIFER LEE
SHANE MORRIS

ORIGINAL SONGS BY
KRISTEN ANDERSON-LOPEZ
AND
ROBERT LOPEZ

ORIGINAL SCORE COMPOSED BY
CHRISTOPHE BECK

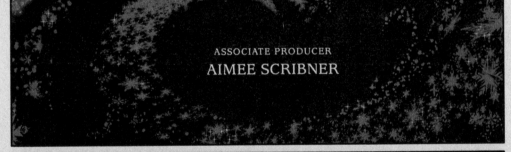

ASSOCIATE PRODUCER
AIMEE SCRIBNER

EDITOR
JEFF DRAHEIM

VISUAL EFFECTS SUPERVISOR
STEVE GOLDBERG

ART DIRECTOR
MICHAEL GIAIMO

ASSISTANT ART DIRECTOR
LISA KEENE

PRODUCTION DESIGNER
DAVID WOMERSLEY

CHARACTER DESIGN SUPERVISOR
BILL SCHWAB

PRODUCTION MANAGER
NICOLE P. HEARON

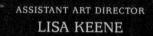

HEAD OF STORY
PAUL BRIGGS

HEAD OF ANIMATION
LINO DI SALVO

DIRECTOR OF
CINEMATOGRAPHY,
LAYOUT
SCOTT BEATTIE

DIRECTOR OF
CINEMATOGRAPHY,
LIGHTING
MOHIT KALLIANPUR

TECHNICAL SUPERVISOR
MARK HAMMEL

CHARACTER CG SUPERVISOR
FRANK HANNER

MODELING SUPERVISOR, CHARACTERS
CHAD STUBBLEFIELD

MODELING SUPERVISOR, ENVIRONMENTS
JON KIM KRUMMEL II

LOOK SUPERVISOR, CHARACTERS
MICHELLE LEE ROBINSON

LOOK SUPERVISOR, ENVIRONMENTS
HANS-JOERG E. KEIM

CHARACTER TD SUPERVISOR, SIMULATION
KEITH WILSON

CHARACTER TD SUPERVISORS, RIGGING
CARLOS CABRAL
GREGORY SMITH

TECHNICAL ANIMATION SUPERVISOR
MARK EMPEY

EFFECTS SUPERVISORS
DALE MAYEDA
MARLON WEST

STEREOSCOPIC SUPERVISOR

KATIE A. FICO

ANIMATION SUPERVISORS

REBECCA WILSON BRESEE
HYRUM VIRL OSMOND
MALCON B. PIERCE III
TONY SMEED
WAYNE UNTEN

LIGHTING SUPERVISORS

ALESSANDRO JACOMINI
HANS-JOERG E. KEIM
RICHARD E. LEHMANN
JASON MacLEOD
ROBERT L. MILES
AMOL SATHE
JOSH STAUB

ASSOCIATE TECHNICAL SUPERVISORS
THADDEUS P. MILLER
RICKY RIECKENBERG

EXECUTIVE MUSIC PRODUCER
CHRIS MONTAN

MUSIC SUPERVISOR
TOM MacDOUGALL

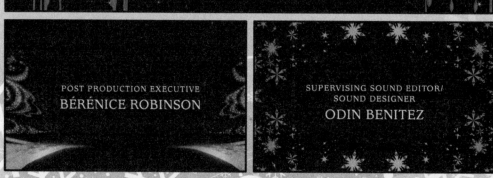

POST PRODUCTION EXECUTIVE
BÉRÉNICE ROBINSON

SUPERVISING SOUND EDITOR/
SOUND DESIGNER
ODIN BENITEZ

CAST

Anna	KRISTEN BELL
Elsa	IDINA MENZEL
Kristoff	JONATHAN GROFF
Olaf	JOSH GAD
Hans	SANTINO FONTANA
Duke	ALAN TUDYK
Pabbie/Grandpa	CIARÁN HINDS
Oaken	CHRIS WILLIAMS
Kai	STEPHEN JOHN ANDERSON
Bulda	MAIA WILSON
Gerda	EDIE McCLURG
Bishop	ROBERT PINE
King	MAURICE LaMARCHE
Young Anna	LIVVY STUBENRAUCH
Young Elsa	EVA BELLA
Teen Elsa	SPENCER GANUS
Spanish Dignitary	JESSE CORTI
German Dignitary	JEFFREY MARCUS
Irish Dignitary	TUCKER GILMORE

Additional Voices

AVA ACRES	STEPHEN APOSTOLINA
ANNALEIGH ASHFORD	KIRK BAILY
JENICA BERGERE	DAVE BOAT
PAUL BRIGGS	TYREE BROWN
WOODY BUCK	JUNE CHRISTOPHER
LEWIS CLEALE	WENDY CUTLER
TERRI DOUGLAS	EDDIE FRIERSON
JEAN GILPIN	JACKIE GONNEAU
NICHOLAS GUEST	BRIDGET HOFFMAN
NICK JAMESON	DANIEL KAZ
JOHN LAVELLE	JENNIFER LEE
PAT LENTZ	ANNIE LOPEZ
KATIE LOWES	MONA MARSHALL
DARA McGARRY	SCOTT MENVILLE
ADAM OVERETT	PAUL PAPE
COURTNEY PELDON	JENNIFER PERRY
RAYMOND S. PERSI	JEAN-MICHEL RICHAUD
LYNWOOD ROBINSON	CARTER SAND
JADON SAND	KATIE SILVERMAN
PEPPER SWEENEY	FRED TATASCIORE

Casting Associate	CYMBRE WALK

Production Finance Lead	BELINDA M. HSU

STORY

Production Supervisor	JESSICA JULIUS

Story Artists

CLIO CHIANG	NORMAND LEMAY
STEVEN MARKOWSKI	NICOLE MITCHELL
RAYMOND S. PERSI	JEFFREY RESOLME RANJO
JOHN RIPA	MARC SMITH
FAWN VEERASUNTHORN	CHRIS WILLIAMS

Additional Story Artists

STEPHEN ANDERSON	KELLY ASBURY
DON DOUGHERTY	TOM ELLERY
NATHAN GRENO	KEVIN HARKEY
KENDELLE HOYER	BARRY JOHNSON
MARK KENNEDY	JEREMY SPEARS
CHRIS URE	DEAN WELLINS

Additional Story by	KRISTEN ANDERSON-LOPEZ
Story Apprentice	JIHYUN PARK
Production Assistants	ASHLEY READ
	ELISE M. L. SCANLAN

EDITORIAL

Production Supervisor	HEATHER BLODGET
First Assistant Editors	ANTHONY DURAZZO
	ERIC WHITFIELD
Second Assistant Editor	BRIAN MILLMAN
Dialogue Reader	HERMANN H. SCHMIDT
Additional Editorial Support	RICK HAMMEL
	DANYA JOSEPH
	KAREN WHITE
Production Coordinator	LEAH LATHAM
Production Assistant	MICHELLE McMILLAN

VISUAL DEVELOPMENT

Production Supervisor	JAMES E. HASMAN

Visual Development Artists

JAMES A. FINCH	JIM FINN
MAC GEORGE	JEAN GILLMORE
CLAIRE KEANE	LISA KEENE
JIN KIM	SHIYOON KIM
BRITTNEY LEE	HYUN-MIN LEE
MINKYU LEE	CORY LOFTIS
DAN LUND	BILL PERKINS
JEAN-CHRISTOPHE POULAIN	DOUG WALKER
DAVID WOMERSLEY	VICTORIA YING

Additional Visual Development

SARAH AIRRIESS	SUNNY APINCHAPONG
RUBEN A. AQUINO	DALE L. BAER
ADAM DYKSTRA	BRIAN FERGUSON
ANDY HARKNESS	RANDY HAYCOCK
MARK HENN	JULIA KALANTAROVA
ALEX KUPERSHMIDT	KEVIN NELSON
BRUCE W. SMITH	FRANS VISCHER
LARRY WU	

ASSET PRODUCTION

Production Supervisor, Characters	NATHAN CURTIS
Production Supervisor, Environments	JAMES E. HASMAN

Character TDs, Rigging

JESUS CANAL	IKER J. de los MOZOS
JOY JOHNSON	SCOTT PETERS
NICKLAS PUETZ	MATT SCHILLER
MATT STEELE	DAVID J. SUROVIEC

Character TDs, Simulation

AARON ADAMS	JENNIFER R. DOWNS
ERIK EULEN	AVNEET KAUR
HUBERT LEO	JEFF MacNEILL
CLAUDIA CHUNG SANII	TIMMY TOMPKINS
MARC THYNG	MARY TWOHIG
XINMIN ZHAO	

Modelers

SHAUN ABSHER	CHRISTOPHER ANDERSON
VIRGILIO JOHN AQUINO	NADJA BONACINA
CHARLES CUNNINGHAM-SCOTT	STEFANO DUBAY
DYLAN EKREN	BRIEN HINDMAN
KEVIN HUDSON	HIROKI ITOKAZU
JACKY KE JIANG	SUZAN KIM
LUIS LABRADOR	BRANDON LAWLESS
IRENE MATAR	CHRIS PATRICK O'CONNELL
FLORIAN PERRET	ERIC PROVAN
EDWARD E. ROBBINS III	SAMY SEGURA
JUAN SOLIS GARCIA	RYAN TOTTLE
ALENA WOOTEN TOTTLE	

Production Coordinator	MARISA X. CASTRO
Production Assistants, Characters	ALLISON MARTIN
	KIT TURLEY
Production Assistant, Environments	JASMINE GONZALEZ

LOOK DEVELOPMENT

Production Supervisor	MIKE HUANG
Pre-Production Supervisor	CHUCK TAPPAN
Pre-Production Look Supervisor	RYAN DUNCAN
Look Lead	LANCE SUMMERS

Look Development Artists

ALEXANDER ALVARADO	JOAN ANASTAS
AUDREY BAGLEY	SARA VIRGINIA CEMBALISTY
TRACY LEE CHURCH	CHARLES COLLADAY
PAULA GOLDSTEIN	JOHN HUIKKU
DAVID WILKES KERSEY	CHELSEA LAVERTU
MIA LEE	KONRAD LIGHTNER
VICKY YUTZU LIN	JARED REISWEBER
MITCHELL SNARY	PAMELA SPERTUS
SHERI WONG	

Matte Painter	JANG LEE

Look Development Apprentices

RAMYA CHIDANAND	NIKKI MULL	JOSE LUIS "WEECHO" VELASQUEZ

Look Development TDs

STELLA HSIN-HUEI CHENG	MARC COOPER	PATRICK DALTON
TAL LANCASTER		LEWIS N. SIEGEL

Production Coordinator	CAITLIN PEAK COONS

LAYOUT

Production Supervisor	TUCKER GILMORE
Layout Lead/Camera Polish	CORY ROCCO FLORIMONTE

Layout Artists

JOAQUIN BALDWIN	ALLEN BLAISDELL
DANIEL HU	KEVIN LEE
TERRY MOEWS	RICK MOORE
MERRICK RUSTIA	MATSUNE SUZUKI
KENDRA VANDER VLIET	DAVID WAINSTAIN
DOUG WALKER	NATHAN DETROIT WARNER

Layout Apprentices	TYLER KUPFERER
	MATT SULLIVAN
Layout Trainee	SCOTT ARMSTRONG
Layout Finaling Artists	CELESTE JOANETTE
	TAMARA ALEJANDRA FARALLA KERSAVAGE
	MICHAEL TALARICO
Layout TDs	MIKE HARRIS
	JEFF SADLER
	SHWETA VISWANATHAN
Production Coordinator	ALBERT V. RAMIREZ
Production Assistant	ALLISON MARTIN

ANIMATION

Production Supervisor	ANGELA FRANCES D'ANNA
Lead 2D Animator	MARK HENN

Animators

ALBERTO ABRIL	VALENTIN AMADOR DIAZ	BERT KLEIN	MICHAEL KLIM
DOUG BENNETT	JOEY BROWN	DANIEL JAMES KLUG	MATT KUMMER
DARRIN BUTTERS	ANDREW CHESWORTH	ANDREW LAWSON	HYUN-MIN LEE
YOUNGJAE CHOI	CHRISTOPHER CORDINGLEY	KIRA LEHTOMAKI	KEVIN MacLEAN
STEVE CUNNINGHAM	AMANDA DAGUE	STEPHANE MANGIN	KELLY McCLANAHAN
PATRICK DANAHER	RENATO DOS ANJOS	BRIAN F. MENZ	MATTHEW MEYER
JEFFREY ENGEL	CHADD FERRON	MARK MITCHELL	MARLON NOWE
JASON FIGLIOZZI	MICHAEL FRANCESCHI	DANIEL MARTÍN PEIXE	BOBBY PONTILLAS
DEREK FRIESENBORG	MINOR JOSE GAYTAN	NICOLAS PROTHAIS	MITJA RABAR
RYAN GONG	STEVEN PIERRE GORDON	JOEL REID	BURKE ROANE
ADAM GREEN	JENNIFER HAGER	BRIAN SCOTT	CHAD SELLERS
RYAN HOBBIEBRUNKEN	ROBERT HUTH	BENSON SHUM	JUSTIN SKLAR
DARRELL JOHNSON	MACK KABLAN	AMY LAWSON SMEED	BILL TESSIER
JOHN KAHRS	MIYUKI KANNO LONG	GEOFF WHEELER	MARK A. WILLIAMS
CLAY KAYTIS	MICHEAL KIELY	JOHN WONG	KATHY ZIELINSKI

Animating Assistants

RIANNON DELANOY   MARAT DAVLETSHIN
MARIO FURMANCZYK   DANIEL GONZALES III
SVETLA RADIVOEVA   RASTKO STEFANOVIĆ
MICHAEL WOODSIDE

Animation Apprentices

FRANK E. ABNEY III   ANDREW ATTEBERRY
TONY CHAU   TRENT CORREY
JORGE GARCIA   JORGE E. RUIZ C.
JUSTIN WEBER

Animation TDs   FABRICE CEUGNIET
CHRISTOPHER OTTO GALLAGHER
REBECCA VALLERA-THOMPSON
Production Coordinators   LAURA M. MEREDITH
KIT TURLEY
Production Assistant   JESSICA "JAC" CHEN

TECHNICAL ANIMATION

Production Supervisor   KRISTIN LEIGH YADAMEC

Technical Animation Artists

ARTURO AGUILAR   VIRGILIO JOHN AQUINO
KATHLEEN M. BAILEY   BRET BAYS
COREY BOLWYN   NICHOLAS BURKARD
AARON CAMPBELL   JESUS CANAL
GLEN CLAYBROOK   CASEY DAME
ERIK EULEN   CHRISTOPHER EVART
JAY GAMBELL   ROSE IBIAMA
ANDREW JENNINGS   JOY JOHNSON
WILLIAM D. KASTAK   SI-HYUNG KIM
ADAM REED LEVY   MAIA NEUBIG
NAVIN MARTIN PINTO   BRYAN POON
LUIS SAN JUAN PALLARES   MICHAEL W. STIEBER
DAVID J. SUROVIEC   JOHN TRUONG
RICHARD VAN CLEAVE JR.   ERIC WARREN
ZACK WEILER   WALTER YODER

Production Coordinator   BRANDON HOLMES
Production Assistant   AUSTIN SALMI

CROWD ANIMATION

Production Supervisor   KRISTIN LEIGH YADAMEC
Crowd Lead   MOE EL-ALI
Crowd Artists   ERIN J. ELLIOTT
JOHN MURRAH
TUAN NGUYEN
Additional Crowd Artist   YASSER HAMED
Production Coordinator   BRANDON HOLMES
Production Assistant   AUSTIN SALMI

EFFECTS

Production Supervisor   LESLEY ADDARIO BENTIVEGNA
Effects Designers   IAN J. COONY
DAN LUND

Effects Animators

MIR ALI   JUSTIN ANDREWS
ERIC W. ARAUJO   BOB BENNETT
BRETT BOGGS   MARC BRYANT
DONG JOO BYUN   CHRIS CARIGNAN
MICHAEL CHAPMAN   ERIC DANIELS
JESSE ERICKSON   BENJAMIN FISKE
BEN FROST   CHRISTOPHER HENDRYX
DAVID HUTCHINS   JOHN HUGHES
SAM KLOCK   JOHN KOSNIK
JAMES DeV. MANSFIELD   TIM MOLINDER
DAN NAULIN   MIKE NAVARRO
HENDRIK PANZ   BLAIR PIERPONT
DAVE RAND   BRIAN SILVA
KEE NAM SUONG   ZUBIN WADIA
THOMAS WICKES   BRUCE WRIGHT
JAE HYUN YOO   XIAO ZHANG

Effects TDs   TONY CHAI
VIJOY GADDIPATI
NEELIMA KARANAM
Effects Apprentices   SHAN DUAN
RATTANIN SIRINARUEMARN
Additional Effects   LAWRENCE CHAI
ALEXEY DMITRIEVICH STOMAKHIN
Production Coordinator   MELISSA GENOSHE
Production Assistant   MATT SCHIAVONE

LIGHTING

Production Supervisor   SHERI PATTERSON

Lighting Artists

JOAN ANASTAS   SALVADOR ARDITTI   DAN LEVY   BENJAMIN LISHKA
JASON BARLOW   JEFFREY BENEDICT   VINA KAO MAHONEY   JONATHAN FLETCHER MOORE
KEN BRAIN   COREY BUTLER   CRISTIAN G. MORAS   CHRIS NABHOLZ
ONNY CARR   JEFF CHUNG   DEREK NELSON   JAMES NEWLAND
GREGORY CULP   CHERYL DAVIS   ALEX NIJMEH   STEPHEN NULL
RYAN DeYOUNG   JUSTIN DOBIES   EILEEN O'NEILL   JORGE OBREGON
KAORI DOI   SHANT ERGENIAN   AMY PFAFFINGER   ELLEN POON
JOSH FRY   ALEX GARCIA   ALAN PRECOURT   WINSTON QUITASOL
LOGAN GLOOR   PAULA GOLDSTEIN   KATIE REIHMAN   DANIEL RICE
RICHARD GOUGE   BENJAMIN MIN HUANG   OLLIN RILEY   FRANK A. SABIA JR.
ADRIAN ILER   KATHERINE IPJIAN   WALLY SCHAAB   ROBERT SHOWALTER
IVA ITCHEVSKA-BRAIN   ARTHUR JEPPE   MARK SIEGEL   KA YAW TAN
JONGO   BLAINE KENNISON   FATEMA TARZI   EMILY TSE
HOLLY KIM-ANGEL   MacDUFF KNOX   ELIZABETH WILLY   FARID YAZAMI
KEVIN KONEVAL   DAN KRUSE   JENNIFER YU   NASHEET ZAMAN
GINA LAWES   ROGER LEE   DIANA J. ZENG

Lighting Apprentices
JEFF GIPSON   MOHANNED HASSAN
KYLE HUMPHREY   RYAN CHRISTOPHER LANG
ANGELA McBRIDE

Lighting TDs
DEXTER CHENG   KAY CLOUD
ALLEN CORCORRAN   ANDREW P. GARTNER
KIMBERLY W. KEECH   HEATHER PRITCHETT

Assistant TDs
MAURICIO GOMEZ AGUINAGA   SARA DRAKELEY
SEAN FLYNN   KELSEY HURLEY
NADIM SINNO

Production Coordinators   MARISA X. CASTRO
STEPH GORTZ
LAUREN LEFFINGWELL
Production Assistants   DEREK MANZELLA
ASHLEY READ

STEREO

Production Supervisor   JULIE BANER

Stereo Artists
MICHAEL R. W. ANDERSON   THOMAS BAKER
ANITA EDWARDS   TROY GRIFFIN
MARK HENLEY   TINA-LORRAINE RANGEL
VANESSA SALAS CASTILLO   DARREN SIMPSON

Stereo Assistants
HEIDI FRIESE   LAUREN KRAMER   FELIPE RUIZ REYES
Production Assistant   JORDAN BEDER-SCHENKER

 ## PRODUCTION

Production Supervisors, Publicity   JAMES E. HASMAN
DARA McGARRY
Production Assistant, Publicity   JASMINE GONZALEZ
Production Supervisor, Sweatbox   JULIE BANER
Production Assistant, Sweatbox   JORDAN BEDER-SCHENKER
Assistant to Producer   ERIN SENGE
Assistant to Directors   HALIMA HUDSON
Shotgun Software Specialist   PAUL FIEHIGER
Production Finance Analyst   JENNIFER "JEJO" SLEEPER

ADDITIONAL PRODUCTION SUPPORT

LINDSAY HENRY   DAVE KOHUT   ADRIENNE BLAIR VALLANCE

MUSIC

Original Songs Produced by   KRISTEN ANDERSON-LOPEZ
ROBERT LOPEZ
Original Score Produced by   JAKE MONACO
Songs Recorded and Mixed by   DAVID BOUCHER
Score Recorded and Mixed by   CASEY STONE
Songs Orchestrated by   DAVID METZGER
Score Orchestrations by   KEVIN KLIESCH
DAVID METZGER
TIM DAVIES
Songs Conducted by   STEPHEN OREMUS
Score Conducted by   TIM DAVIES
Music Production Director   ANDREW PAGE
Music Editor, Production Songs   EARL GHAFFARI
Music Editor, Score   FERNAND BOS
Music Business Affairs   DONNA COLE-BRULE
Music Production Coordinator   ASHLEY CHAFIN
Executive Music Assistant   JILL HEFFLEY
Music Production Assistant   JIMMY TSAI
Vocal Coaching by   SAM KRIGER
Additional Song Orchestrations by   CHRISTOPHE BECK
STEPHEN OREMUS
DOUG BESTERMAN
Additional Song Recording by   KEVIN HARP
JOEY RAIA
Score Digital Recordist   LARRY MAH
Score Coordinators   LEO BIRENBERG
ZACH ROBINSON
Score Technical Engineer   TOM HARDISTY
Technical Assistants   RYAN ROBINSON
RICHARD WHEELER JR.
Songs Contracted by   REGGIE WILSON
Score Contracted by   PETER ROTTER
Score Choir Contracted by   JASPER RANDALL
Music Preparation by   BOOKER WHITE - WALT DISNEY MUSIC
JoANN KANE MUSIC SERVICE

"FROZEN HEART"   "DO YOU WANT TO BUILD A SNOWMAN?"
Performed by   Performed by Kristen Bell, Agatha Lee Monn
Cast   and Katie Lopez

"FOR THE FIRST TIME IN FOREVER"   "LOVE IS AN OPEN DOOR"
Performed by   Performed by
Kristen Bell and Idina Menzel   Kristen Bell and Santino Fontana

"LET IT GO"   "REINDEER(S) ARE BETTER THAN PEOPLE"
Performed by Idina Menzel   Performed by Jonathan Groff

"IN SUMMER"   "FOR THE FIRST TIME IN FOREVER (Reprise)"
Performed by Josh Gad   Performed by
Kristen Bell and Idina Menzel

"FIXER UPPER"
Performed by Maia Wilson and Cast   "LET IT GO (Demi Lovato Version)"
Performed by Demi Lovato
"VUELIE"   Produced by Emanuel "Eman" Kiriakou
and "VUELIE" (Reprise)   and Andrew "Goldstein" Goldstein
Written and Produced by   Mixed by Serban Ghenea
Frode Fjellheim and Christophe Beck   Demi Lovato
Performed by Cantus   appears courtesy of Hollywood Records
Conducted by Tove Ramlo-Ystad

Featured Vocalist (Score) CHRISTINE HALS

POST PRODUCTION

Post Production Supervisor	BRENT W. HALL
Post Production Coordinator	BRYCE OLSON
Original Dialogue Mixers	GABRIEL GUY
	DOC KANE
	BILL HIGLEY
Sound Services	THE WALT DISNEY STUDIOS, BURBANK
	FORMOSA GROUP
Re-Recording Mixers	DAVID E. FLUHR, CAS
	GABRIEL GUY
Supervising Dialogue/ADR Editor	CHRISTOPHER T. WELCH, MPSE
Dialogue Editor	ELIZA POLLACK ZEBERT, MPSE
Supervising Foley Editor	TODD TOON
Foley Editor	CHARLES W. RITTER
Sound Effects Editors	JEFF SAWYER
	ANGELO PALAZZO
	GREGORY HEDGEPATH, MPSE
	MARTYN ZUB
	STEVE ROBINSON
First Assistant Sound Editor	PERNELL L. SALINAS
Foley Artists	JOHN ROESCH
	ALYSON DEE MOORE
Foley Mixer	MARY JO LANG
Mix Technician	BRIAN DINKINS
ADR Group Voice Casting	TERRI DOUGLAS
Digital Imaging Specialist	ROBERT H. BAGLEY
Digital Intermediate Colorist	ELIOT MILBOURN
Domestic Film Color Timer	JIM PASSON
End Titles	SCARLET LETTERS
End Title Art Design	LISA KEENE
	DAVID WOMERSLEY
Transfer Room/Theater Operator	LUTZNER RODRIGUEZ
	GABRIEL STEWART

 ## FILM AND DIGITAL SERVICES

Director	JOE JIULIANO
Manager	SUZY RAUCH
Production Administrator	PATRICIA ADEFOLAYAN RIZZO
Supervisor	WILLIAM J. FADNESS
Technical Supervisor	CHRISTOPHER W. GEE
Camera Operator	REZA KASRAVI
Lead Localization Title Artist	BRIAN RISHEL
Localization Title Artist	DAVID FEINNER
CGI Digital Artist	KYLE STRAWITZ

 ## TECHNOLOGY

Technology Directors	DAN CANDELA
	JONATHAN E. GEIBEL

ANIMATION TECHNOLOGY

Technology Manager	EVAN GOLDBERG
Principal Software Engineer	MARK A. McLAUGHLIN

MATT JEN-YUAN CHIANG	JOSE LUIS GOMEZ DIAZ	CATHERINE LAM
GENE S. LEE	CHUNG-AN ANDY LIN	ANDY MILNE
DMITRIY PINSKIY	JAY STEELE	ALEXANDRE D. TORIJA-PARIS
JUSTIN WALKER		BRIAN WHITED

LOOK/EFFECTS/DYNAMICS

Technology Manager	RAJESH SHARMA
Principal Software Engineers	DAVID M. ADLER
	ANDREW SELLE

DAVID AGUILAR	LAWRENCE CHAI
YING LIU	ALEKA McADAMS
MARYANN SIMMONS	ALEXEY DMITRIEVICH STOMAKHIN
DANIEL TEECE	KELLY WARD HAMMEL

INTERACTION DESIGN

JANET E. BERLIN	JOEL EDEN
KRISPIN J. LEYDON	MATTHEW E. LEVINE
Technology Trainee	NARA YUN

MEDIA ENGINEERING

Principal Media Engineer	PATRICK DANFORD

JASON L. BERGMAN	JEFFREY R. CORNISH
GLENN DAKAKE	NORBERT FAERSTAIN
TARALYN ROSE FRASQUERI-MOLINA	JEFFREY L. SICKLER
KAMALDEEP TUMKUR SRINATH	JAMES A. WARGOWSKI

PIPELINE/ENGINEERING SERVICES

Technology Manager	DARREN ROBINSON
Principal Software Engineers	BRENT BURLEY
	TODD SCOPIO

WILLIAM T. CARPENTER	CHRISTIAN EISENACHER	YUN-PO PAUL FAN
ANDREW FISHER	NOAH KAGAN	ERIC BUUS LARSEN
DOUGLAS E. LESAN	JOHN LONGHINI	JOSEPH W. LONGSON
GREG NICHOLS	GARRET SAKURA	LISA S. YOUNG
TAMARA VALDES	MEGHAN VELTRI	HOWARD WILCZYNSKI

SPECIAL THANKS

DR. KARL BIRKELAND	JACKSON CRAWFORD	DANILO
DR. JEFF DOZIER	MICHAEL GOI, ASC	DAVID GOLDSTEIN
THEIS DUELAND JENSEN	DIANA KURIYAMA	DR. KENNETH LIBBRECHT
WARNER LOUGHLIN	CRAIG SCHROEDER	JOSEPH M. TERAN

EINAR AASEN	CYNTHIA BALLARDO	CLAUDIA BATCKE
LEROY BECKER	BJØRG BJØBERG	INGER CARTER
TRACY FARHAD	BRIAN GALE	THOMAS GRANDE
MAGNE EGGEN HAUGOM	JAMES P. HURRELL	ESTHER JACOBSEN BATES
LESLIE JAMES	RUNE JOHANSEN	STINE ELISABETH JOHANSEN
MICHAEL KASCHALK	KENNETH KENYON	KURT OVE LIDAL
RICK MARZULLO	KARL MJELVA	ANNEKRISTIN MOE
ELLING NIDENG	EVA NORDFJELL	ROSANNA PADOIN
DR. THOMAS "DR. SNOW" PAINTER	BEATE ALBRIGTSEN PEDERSEN	GUNHILD REINSKOU
LYNWOOD ROBINSON	SAGE THE REINDEER	GEORGE STUART
THOMAS V. THOMPSON II	ØYSTEIN USTVEDT	BRIAN WHERRY
	PHIL'S ANIMAL RENTALS	

THE SCIENCE & ENTERTAINMENT EXCHANGE

PRODUCTION BABIES

ALEXANDRA	ALVARO	ANNIKA	ARDEN "HA-YEON"	ASHER
BRIAR	CALEB	CHARLOTTE	CLARA	CODY
ELIAS	EVERETT	EVEY	HIKARI	IVY
JEREMY	JOLIANNA	JULIAN	LIAM	LINCOLN
LUKE	NATHAN	NATHANIEL	OLIVER	OLIVER
PERI	PETRA	PROSPER	ROMAN	SARAH
SLOANE	THOMAS		TROUPE	WEDNESDAY

The views and opinions expressed by Kristoff in the film that all men eat their own boogers
are solely his own and do not necessarily reflect the views or opinions of
The Walt Disney Company or the filmmakers. Neither The Walt Disney Company
nor the filmmakers make any representation of the accuracy of any such views and opinions.

Original Soundtrack Available on

Video Games Available From

Prints by DELUXE®

Distributed by
WALT DISNEY STUDIOS MOTION PICTURES

THE MAGIC IS BACK!

RELIVE THE WONDER THIS HOLIDAY SEASON WITH **BIG** Disney GRAPHIC NOVEL COLLECTIONS, ONLY FROM JOE BOOKS!

ALL THE GRACE, ALL THE WONDER, ONE EPIC BOOK!

For years, Disney's Princesses have charmed audiences the world over in their spellbinding animated films, winning the day with wit and pluck as the power of love keeps the darkness at bay. Return to these thrilling worlds of magic, danger and romance in this timeless graphic novel collection from Disney's own master artists. Every Disney Princess film is retold in this 800-page storytime treasure that Princess fans will cherish for a lifetime.

STORIES INCLUDE

- Snow White
- Cinderella
- Sleeping Beauty
- The Little Mermaid
- Beauty and the Beast
- Aladdin
- Pocahontas
- Mulan
- Princess and the Frog
- Tangled
- Brave

Disney
PRINCESS
COMICS TREASURY

800 PAGES OF MAGICAL ADVENTURES!

COVER NOT FINAL

DISNEY PRINCESS TREASURY
BY DISNEY ARTISTS AND WRITERS
6 X 9 / FULL-COLOR / 800 PAGES / AGES 8 TO 12
PAPERBACK UPC: 627843434795 / $19.99/$24.99 CAN
PUBLISHED BY JOE BOOKS
ON SALE DECEMBER 3, 2014

THE MAGIC IS BACK!

RELIVE THE WONDER THIS HOLIDAY SEASON WITH *BIG* Disney GRAPHIC NOVEL COLLECTIONS, ONLY FROM JOE BOOKS!

ALL THE HEART, ALL THE [AD]VENTURE, ONE EPIC BOOK!

[M]ike and Sully, Buzz and Woody, Lightning [McQueen] and Mater — relive their thrilling stories [a]nd more in this giant-sized graphic novel treasury featuring all of your favorite Disney•Pixar friends. Every classic film from the legendary animation studio is [r]etold here in vibrant comics that jump off [t]he page, drawn by Disney's own master [a]rtists. With 800 pages of excitement, the [DI]SNEY•PIXAR OMNIBUS is a must-have for any Disney•Pixar fan's collection!

STORIES INCLUDE
- Toy Story 1, 2 & 3
- A Bug's Life
- Monsters, Inc. & Monsters University
- Finding Nemo
- The Incredibles
- Cars & Cars 2
- Ratatouille
- Wall•E
- Up

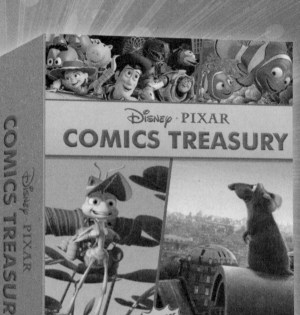

COVER NOT FINAL

DISNEY•PIXAR TREASURY
BY DISNEY ARTISTS AND WRITERS
6 X 9 / FULL-COLOR / 800 PAGES / AGES 8 TO 12
PAPERBACK UPC: 627843434788 / $19.99/$24.99 CAN
PUBLISHED BY JOE BOOKS
ON SALE DECEMBER 3, 2014